THE THREE SISTERS TRILOGY BOOK 3

TANGLEWOOD LEGACY

USA TODAY BESTSELLING AUTHOR
GENEVIEVE JACK

Tanglewood Legacy: The Three Sisters, Book 3

Copyright © Genevieve Jack 2022

Published by Carpe Luna Ltd, Bloomington, IL 61704

First Edition: March 2021

Cover art by Deranged Doctor Designs

eISBN: 978-1-940675-80-0

Paperback: 978-1-940675-81-7

v 3.0

ABOUT THIS BOOK

She's his greatest discovery and about to become his greatest challenge.

En route to New Orleans with her sisters, Isis Tanglewood wakes in the middle of the night to memories of a demon. Nothing surprises her more than to find shipmate Delphine has also dreamed of the same monster. After their brief encounter, Delphine begs Isis to help her and her sisters avoid forced marriages in New Orleans. Isis empathizes but refuses her for fear of drawing attention to her family's witchy secret.

Scientist and philosopher Pierre Baron lives to map the stars from his observatory and to research the natural history of the burgeoning colony in Louisiana he calls home. But when he meets Isis, his curiosity is piqued like never before. Magic happens when he makes it his mission to learn more about her, and he soon determines she's just as curious about him.

When a man is found dead on the banks of the Mississippi, drained of all his blood, Isis believes a vampire has come to New Orleans. With Pierre's help, she soon comes to suspect Delphine. Isis is a powerful witch and a resourceful woman, but she becomes vulnerable in ways she never expected. Pierre's greatest discovery is his love for Isis, but can he, an ordinary human man, protect her from mystic forces hell-bent on revenge?

CHAPTER ONE

I sis Tanglewood jackknifed off the bed as two glowing red eyes faded from her memory. The nightmare again. She held her head, wiping tears she couldn't remember shedding from under her eyes. She'd been crying in her sleep again. Ever since she'd raised Medea from the dead, she'd suffered dreams that left her heart pounding and her breath short. Dreams that were more than dreams if she was honest with herself. The worst part was, she couldn't even seek out the comfort of her sisters. How could she tell Medea that when she'd descended into Hades to resurrect her, accidentally leaving her unborn son behind, that something else, something *evil*, had taken notice of her and now haunted her at night?

She had enough trouble looking Medea in the eye. Could she ever forgive herself for that terrible mistake? Phineas. Oh goddess, Medea had planned to name the boy Phineas.

Throwing back the covers, she leaped from her bed and rushed to the chamber pot. Her heart beat a mad tattoo within her chest, her stomach somersaulting in the wavering room. Wait, that wasn't in her head. Isis remembered she was on a ship bound for *La Nouvelle-Orléans,* or as the English called it, New Orleans. The sickness she was feeling wasn't from her nightmares at all, but from the roiling of the wooden vessel on the mighty sea.

She grabbed her robe and slipped it on over her nightgown, then flung open the door to her quarters and headed for the upper deck. She needed air. Needed to see the stars, feel the comforting witness of the moon, and connect with the magic that night breathed into her.

Shadows gathered around her ankles. The darkness was trying to comfort her as it always did when she was anxious. Only, for the first time in her life, their presence wasn't entirely welcome. The darkness in her nightmare—the demon with the red eyes—also commanded shadows, and with the memory of his presence fresh in her mind, the tendrils that snaked around her calves felt too much like his touch.

As her bare feet fell on the wooden deck and the warm sea air blew back her dark hair, Isis tried to put the demon out of her mind. The dream was always the same. He wanted her. Wanted to be with her. And the worst part was, as horrifying a visage as the demon possessed, the dream filled her with lust as certainly as it filled her with fear. This particular demon knew how to turn on the charm.

She looked out over the railing toward the singular moon, so different from the night sky of Ouros, and wondered if there was a spell to protect her from her own mind. Her own guilt.

"You too? Bad dreams?" A woman's voice came from behind her, and Isis whirled. She understood the woman's French clearly enough, but her accent was different from what she'd picked up in Provence. *Paris*, she guessed. The woman had the dark curly hair and gray eyes of many she'd met from that region.

"Yes. Is it obvious?" Isis asked.

The woman pulled her robe tighter around her slight frame. She was too thin and too pale, hair dull. Isis had seen it before in other travelers. The sickness took hold, extinguishing the spark in their eyes before slowly draining them of life. "I only assumed as that is why I came up. I think it's the sea. The roiling of the boat does something to my mind. I've never slept well, not one night since we've been on this bloody boat." She arched an eyebrow. "I'm Delphine, by the way. Delphine Devereaux."

"*Enchante*, Delphine. How is it we haven't met before? Have you been in Haiti long?"

"Only long enough to switch vessels. Our original ship is returning to France," Delphine said.

When Isis had set off from Provence with her sisters and Rhys, they'd intended to travel straight to America, but a storm had blown their ship off course, and they'd initially ended up in Haiti. They'd stayed for several months, until once again, their subtle use of magic started to call attention to them. They took no precautions but were never ill. They had no servants, yet their home was always well tended. Food appeared on their table although they employed no cook. Eventually people started to notice, and the whispers became more heated.

Suspicion alone, though, wasn't enough to drive them on. It was the baby. Circe's pregnancy had advanced. Among their kind, babies were notorious for unexpected magic. They needed a place far away from the bustling crowd, a place where they could be safe from human interference.

"You didn't mention your name," Delphine said, shaking her from her thoughts.

"Oh, excuse me. I'm Isis Tanglewood." She gave the woman a shallow curtsy.

"What an unusual name for a French woman," Delphine said. "You are French, are you not?"

"From Provence." Isis shifted uncomfortably. The secret to a good lie was a partial truth. "My mother heard the name while traveling."

Delphine studied her. "And your destination is la Nouvelle-Orléans?" She scoffed, scanning Isis from head to toe. "Did they find you in a brothel or a convent? With skin like yours, I assume a convent."

Isis attempted to tamp down her offense. She was aware that most of the women on this ship were, in fact, taken from brothels, convents, and prisons and offered new lives as wives to hardened colonists of the territory of Louisiana. This Delphine meant no harm in her inquiry. While men might have many reasons for traveling to the Americas, the women here did not share the social freedoms she'd enjoyed in Darnuith before they'd fled her home world. Still, she couldn't bring herself to lie about this.

"Neither," she said honestly. "My sisters and I wanted to settle somewhere new." When Delphine gave her a strange look, she added. "We travel with my sister's husband, Rhys."

Delphine's mouth opened, and she nodded her understanding. A man explained everything. Isis had to keep herself from rolling her eyes. The culture in this dimension was strange, indeed.

"I too travel with my sisters, Lucienne and Antoinette," Delphine said, smiling bitterly. "No husbands, though. I am told we will stay in a convent under the watch of the Ursuline nuns until a suitable match can be made for us. By suitable match, I presume they mean the highest bidder. Whoever is willing to pay for a wife to cook, clean, and warm their bed. After living in the wilds these years, I bet it's the bed-warming they're most in need of, or they wouldn't have sought us out."

Isis frowned. Three sisters, just like them, sold like chattel. The thought upset her, but this was how this realm worked, and there was nothing she could do about the women's fate. "I wish you the best possible outcome."

Delphine opened her mouth to speak but was silenced by a fit of coughing, her face growing paler with her breathlessness until it rivaled the glow of the moon. When she finally stopped, her bottom lip was stained bright red from fresh blood.

The woman was dying. Isis recognized the signs of the illness the people here called consumption. Rhys had the herbs and magic to cure it, but asking him to do so was out of the question. They'd left Provence and then Saint-Domingue to escape scrutiny. What would be the point if they made the same mistakes here and garnered more accusations of witchcraft?

Still, her heart grew heavy, thinking of the woman's plight. By the way she spoke so freely of warming a man's bed, Isis did not doubt that she likely came from a brothel. She feared Delphine's life had been hard and was about to get harder.

Delphine examined her in the moonlight, coughing again into her hand. Her eyes narrowed. "How is it that after weeks of travel, your skin still glows as if it's lit from within? Your figure hasn't suffered a bit from the gruel they serve us. Your hair shines like a raven's wing."

Isis thought quickly. It would not benefit her or her sisters for their relative health to be questioned. "My sisters and I spent several months with friends on a plantation in Saint-Domingue, regaining our strength after the long journey from France." Isis raised her chin.

"Ah." She scoffed, and Isis saw her eyes turn hard. "A proper lady with friends in high places. Perhaps I shouldn't be speaking so openly above my class." The harsh sting of her tone told her that Delphine didn't think highly of proper ladies.

"I'm quite certain a proper lady wouldn't be on a ship to the wilds of America." Isis heaved a beleaguered sigh. "I hope we can be friends once you've made your new home, Delphine."

The sickly woman made a guttural sound. "Of course. Now, if you'll excuse me, I find I've grown tired again. Sleep well, Isis." She gave a shallow curtsy and headed for the stairs.

"Delphine?" Isis called, suddenly curious at the talk of sleep. The woman paused her descent and looked at her expectantly. "What was *your* nightmare about?"

The woman smiled a mouth of yellowing teeth. "I dreamed of a red-eyed demon," she said, then grinned wider. "I just hope it wasn't my future husband."

Isis hugged herself against an unexpected chill as Delphine disappeared below deck.

CHAPTER
TWO

"The air feels like a damp wool blanket fresh from the boiling cauldron," Isis said, whispering an incantation to cool herself. "No wonder they need to ship wives in for the men here. La Nouvelle-Orléans has the same climate as the threshold of Hades."

Circe laughed, rubbing her protruding belly. "Try it pregnant. I feel like I'm burning up from the inside out. Still, it's no worse than Saint-Domingue. This is where we belong. I've seen it."

"I've seen it too," Isis agreed.

"Careful, sisters," Medea said in hushed tones, glancing at the crowd disembarking from the ship and gathering on the wooden plank walkway. "Magic is rolling off you like perfume. Let's not announce ourselves as witches quite so soon. This parish is far less settled than France, but we can assume their stakes and their witches burn just as well."

Rhys adjusted the Tanglewood tree in his arms. "The land grant I procured in Haiti is for a plot several miles north, along the Mississippi. We'll need horses, and I am to

7

visit with a man in the *Vieux Carré* to finalize the arrangement."

"What about the trunks?" Isis asked, glancing back toward the ship.

Medea flourished a hand toward the large leather satchel on her shoulder. "Minimization spell. Wholly reversible."

"Genius." Isis noticed the crowd was moving in a common direction. "I'd guess the old square is that way. I'm sure everything we need is there."

"What are they doing with those women?" Circe asked. She pointed at a group of austere-looking nuns not far from them, dressed in long black dresses with stiff white panels at their necks and heads topped in black veils. The outfits looked miserable in the heat but made it impossible to miss the religious order. They stood out and commanded attention. Between them was a small group of haggard-looking ladies, each carrying chests that Isis assumed contained their personal belongings. Although they must not have much if that was their only luggage.

"Wives for the colonists. The men are already gathering." Medea pointed to a crowd of rowdy men beyond the nuns. Isis's heart filled with pity for the women. With leathery skin and sweaty shirts, the men looked uncivilized and disorderly, pushing and shoving one another to take long and lascivious looks at the women, whistling and shouting obscenities. Their raucous laughter and bawdy humor were cause for chastisement by the nuns, but the men seemed to take no mind of them.

One especially brutish man with wild brown hair pulled a knife and held it to another man's throat for some unheard provocation. After a brief scuffle that thankfully didn't draw blood, the knife-wielding man prevailed, sending the other running.

"Is that a fleur-de-lis on his forearm?" Circe asked, indicating the man with the knife.

Isis narrowed her eyes, trying to make out the mark from a distance, and finally employed a bit of magic to see better. "He's been branded."

Medea nodded. "The fleur-de-lis? A former prisoner, then. I'd heard many were sent here to help settle the land for France."

"Positively vile." Isis smoothed her skirts. "Fine neighbors I'm sure they will be."

The smile Medea gave her was filled with mirth. "Come now, Isis, *we* are the wickedest thing that could possibly walk these streets."

Isis couldn't help but grin back. "Inarguably."

A hand landed on her arm, and Isis turned to find Delphine, ghost-white and panicked, behind her. "Mademoiselle Tanglewood, might you need a maid or someone to cook for you? My sister would make a talented servant. She has experience—"

Medea removed Delphine's hand from her elbow before Isis could say a word. "We have no need, but thank you for your offer."

Delphine's eyes grew wider, more flustered as she took in the men gathered on shore. "Please..." Two women came up behind her, their trunks in tow. Isis pressed a hand into her stomach. These must be her sisters, Lucienne and Antoinette. All three women looked terrified, but the youngest one, a petite blonde with large blue eyes, seemed particularly horrified by the pick of husband material. Or perhaps it was her age. She was barely more than a child. Too young to be married.

"Please, Isis. I beg of you," Delphine said, bowing her head slightly. "I do not ask for myself. My sister Antoinette is not suited for this type of... arrangement." She gestured to the men, who, even to Isis, seemed exceptionally depraved, some touching themselves as they gawked.

The desperation in the woman's tone broke her heart, and Isis sent a questioning glance in the direction of Medea, Circe, and Rhys. But it went without saying that having the non-magical living and working among them was counter-productive to what they hoped to achieve here. Rhys flashed her a pitying look but raised an eyebrow as if to say he was behind his wife and Medea completely on the matter. All three shook their heads almost immediately. It was simply impossible, especially considering the baby would be coming soon.

Reaching into her purse, Isis pulled out a few coins, enough to feed a family for a week, and pressed them into Delphine's palm. "I'm sorry. I have no work for you, but please take this. I hope it helps you get your start here."

A nun arrived then and gripped Delphine's arm in one knotted hand. "Come, my children. It will be all right. Come now."

Delphine and her sisters were whisked away toward the other females, but there was no gratitude in her expression for the coins. Delphine looked at Isis with the betrayed and dangerous expression of a wolf whose leg was caught in a trap.

"Did you know her?" Circe asked in a whisper.

"We met on the ship."

"The look she gave you was... chilling," Medea added.

Isis gave a heavy sigh. "She and her sisters were forced to come here to act as wives to those men, I assume in order to avoid prison. I don't think they've had many options in life, and I'm sure Delphine took one look at those men and feared for her youngest sister."

"I understand your compassion for them, but if we've learned anything through our experiences in this realm," Medea said, "it's that we can't interfere. This world has its ways. We have ours."

After everything, Isis agreed with her sister, but she couldn't quite shake the feeling of guilt that hung with her as they made their way toward the Vieux Carré. Not doing anything made her feel helpless, an admittedly useless emotion she'd felt all too often lately. Strange, uncomfortable response considering her significant power.

Without another word, they made their way through the grid of streets. When Rhys spotted the Office of the Intendant, he handed the Tanglewood tree to Medea. A few leaves fell off the branches and drifted toward her toes. "I'm off to perform my manly responsibilities," he announced, touching the brim of his tricorn hat as he'd seen other men do and heading for the simple wood building.

Isis gave a shallow laugh and glanced toward Circe. "He does love being *the man* among us. I fear Rhys may never come down from the pedestal this society has put him on."

"Oh, but he understands who's really in charge!" Circe laughed wickedly.

A regiment of French soldiers turned the corner and marched past them on the road, presumably toward the *Place d'Armes* they'd passed on the way in from port. Soldiers meant there must be *some* order here. Perhaps Delphine and her sisters would end up married to gentlemen after all.

"I'm going to procure horses," Isis said, wanting to keep busy and not think of the women on the dock.

"We'll come with you," Circe offered.

Isis looked at her very pregnant sister and then at Medea, who was tending the Tanglewood tree, and shook her head. "Someone has to wait here for Rhys. Besides, I don't think we should put the tree at any more risk than necessary."

Medea nodded in agreement. "One for each of us, sister."

BETWEEN THE EMOTIONAL DRAIN FROM HER INTERACTION WITH Delphine, her continued lack of sleep, and the unforgiving heat and humidity, Isis fought a pervasive and interminable exhaustion by the time she reached the stables on the edge of the square where a soldier had told her a man named Martin was selling horses. Even her magic seemed sleepy. The shadows that usually clung to her like favored pets followed her listlessly. She gritted her teeth. Part of the cause was surely the state of the Tanglewood tree. What she needed was a quick transaction so that she and her family could be on their way to their new life and put their roots in the ground, both figuratively and literally.

Monsieur Martin was busy chatting with another customer, so Isis made her way to the corral and studied the horses within. These animals weren't common in Darnuith, where witches preferred to fly on brooms and sleds were frequently pulled by dogs. Paragonians used mountain horses, but their feet and legs were built for climbing. These animals seemed oddly delicate comparatively. How was she to choose an animal?

She glanced back at Martin and his customer. Neither looked very interested in her or her needs. Likely, they thought she was waiting for her husband. She heaved a sigh. These earth-dwellers were becoming terribly predictable.

A dappled gray mare walked up to her and nudged her with her nose. "Well, aren't you friendly, sweet girl." She scratched the horse behind the ears and laughed as it nuzzled her cheek.

"You don't want that one, mademoiselle," a man's voice said from behind her. She turned to get a better look at the source of the comment and had to steady herself on the rail. This was no sweaty drunkard or haggard settler. The Frenchman who passed Martin and the other customer and headed straight for her was remarkably clean, with a straight white smile and a head of well-styled curls the color of coffee grounds. His linen shirt was white and loose-fitting everywhere but in the shoulders, where he was exceptionally broad. She could not help but take notice of the way his breeches and boots suited his form.

She cleared thickness from her throat and found her voice the exact moment he seemed to notice her staring. "*Non*? She seems an exceptionally gentle animal."

He scoffed and came closer, stroking the gray mare's neck. "She is. I'd say she'd make a wonderful pet, but this horse can't pull a cart. Considering you disembarked today, I assume you will need a horse to use for driving as well as riding."

Goddess, it was hot. It took her a moment to gather what he was saying. "How do you know I disembarked today?" She hoped he wasn't one of the men who'd come to scope out potential brides. The idea was repulsive.

"Mind, I'm not a voyeur. I was retrieving a shipment of goods from that ship and just happened to notice you with your, uh..." He gave her a quizzical look and circled two fingers in the air.

"Family," she filled in quickly, relieved it was goods he was after and not a woman. "I am here with my two sisters and my sister Circe's husband." For some strange reason, she had no desire for this man to think she was spoken for.

"You have no husband of your own, then, hmm?" His gaze flicked over her face, down her torso, and back up to meet her eyes.

"No," she said through a coy smile, feeling a strange warmth in her bosom she was unaccustomed to.

The corner of his mouth lifted at this news in a way she found quite pleasing. He took a few steps closer, gesturing toward the gray mare. "The carriage of her head is too low." He pointed at the slope of her neck toward her shoulders. "Her conformation is poor. She'll make a terrible driving horse. If you're lucky enough to get her to pull at all, she'll likely injure herself, and you'll have wasted any small price you pay for her."

"Truly?" Isis squinted at the horse. She had no doubt the stranger was telling the truth. What reason would he have to lie? Now that she examined the animals more closely, the other horses for sale seemed to have far more energy and muscle. With the amount of money in her pockets, she could afford any of them.

"Truly," he answered softly. His gaze lingered on her mouth, and Isis experienced an acute awareness of him, almost as if she were being drawn to him, unable to look away. It wasn't lust. She'd felt lust with the demon in her dreams and was familiar with its heady sensation. This was something else—an intense desire to know him better. Odd.

"In any event, I'll need four," she said, breaking the spell. "One for each of us."

"Smart. In this heat, you must be careful not to overwork a single horse. Still, I wouldn't risk the mare. Perhaps the thoroughbreds there." He cleared his throat. "If you have the means."

"I have the means," she answered quickly. Why was she sharing such a thing with this man? Medea would chastise her for simply entertaining this conversation, let alone sharing their financial status. For all she knew, the man could be a thief.

After a long beat, locked in each other's thrall, he took a deep breath, seeming to break the spell between them. Had she imagined the pull between them or was he as affected as she was? "Forgive me. I've been remiss and haven't introduced myself. I am Pierre Baron." He extended his hand toward her.

"Isis Tanglewood." She slipped her ungloved hand into his.

He lowered his mouth to kiss the back of her hand. At the soft press of his lips, she inhaled deeply, and the shadows seemed to come awake, bending and circling at the feeling he ignited in her. She willed her magic under control. What was it about him that tugged at her innermost spirit, even now when she was hot and exhausted?

"Isis, like the Egyptian goddess."

She raised an eyebrow. "You're familiar?"

"I've read some on the subject. *Enchante*, Isis," he said.

"*Enchante, Monsieur Baron*—" Isis began.

"Pierre, *s'il vous plait*," he corrected.

"Pierre, how is it you know so much about horses?" She flashed him her most charming smile.

He brushed the sleeve of his shirt, although she could see no dust there. "Oh, I am no expert. Only from experience do I know anything. My profession requires the use of a reliable team."

"And what is that profession?"

He smiled roguishly, lowering his chin to look at her through intoxicatingly long lashes. "I'd rather show you than tell you."

Isis didn't have a chance to respond. Martin must have finished with his other customer because he adjusted his wide-brimmed hat and strode to their side, his attention focused entirely on Pierre. "How can I help you today, Monsieur Baron?"

"*Bonjour*, Monsieur Martin. Mademoiselle is interested in four of your best horses," he said, never taking his eyes off Isis.

"Excellent. This gentle mare has taken a liking to you. She's a lovely animal, and I can give her to you at a special price."

As hot as it was, Isis felt the shadows gather around her, cooling her skin. Unlike Pierre, this man could not be trusted. She scented his lies like bad magic. "I will take those four." She pointed to the group Pierre had indicated.

"They are very expensive, mademoiselle. Although, if your intended is willing to pay..." The man stared down at her over a scowl.

Isis felt her anger like ice crystals in her veins. "Name your price."

The amount the man tossed out was three times what she was expecting, but she forced herself to remain impassive. A flick of her wand would make the man more cooperative. She'd only just touched it when she realized she wouldn't need it.

"They aren't worth half that, Martin, and you know it," Pierre said through his teeth. "If you ever want my business again, or my referrals, offer her a fair price."

The man raised an eyebrow. "Or what? If you'd like to travel to Biloxi for a better deal, be my guest."

Pierre stepped in closer to the man. "If I make the trip, it will be for far more than four horses. Perhaps I'll bring back a dozen. I've been thinking about diversifying. Would you enjoy some competition in la Nouvelle-Orléans?"

Isis squelched the urge to laugh. She liked this Pierre. She released her wand and turned back to Monsieur Martin, offering him half what he'd demanded.

Martin scowled. "Not unless you can offer me specie upfront."

Isis wasn't surprised at his demand for cash. Word about a severe shortage of coin in the French colonies brought about by the Spanish control of gold and silver mines in South America had reached her during her travels. She opened her purse and extracted the appropriate amount.

The two men's eyes widened at the heavy clink of the coins as she dropped them into Martin's waiting palm and then turned back to the horses. "Shall I round them up myself?"

And so it was that some half hour later, Isis, with Pierre's offered help, led four horses, dressed in new tack, toward the place where she was to meet her family.

"About my earlier offer," he said. "Perhaps you and your family could join me for coffee or lunch one afternoon?"

Isis didn't miss the death rays Medea was casting her way. "I'm afraid we have much work ahead of us and little time for leisure." The idea of seeing Pierre again made her heart sing, but the thought was folly. "Another time?"

"Of course." He slanted her a curious smile, seeming to soak in the tension between her and her sisters. "If you change your mind, ask for me at Touze's tavern. The owner, Nicolas, knows where to find me."

She gave him a curt nod. "Another time, then."

Abruptly, he took her hand and kissed it again, her skin growing hot at the point of contact. On a whim, Isis pinched one of his hairs with her opposite hand and plucked it quickly from his head, covering what she'd done by pretending to swat a fly. Nonchalantly, she slid the lock of hair into her pocket.

He handed her the horses' reins and retreated to where his horse waited for him, leaving her with an odd yearning she didn't understand. Thankfully, Rhys came out of the general store, arms laden with packages, and Isis turned her full attention on the next steps of their journey.

CHAPTER
THREE

P ierre rode toward his home more distracted than he'd ever been. He was, after all, a man of science, normally logical, analytical, not often preoccupied with flights of fancy. But when he'd seen her standing by the horses and she'd introduced herself as Isis—by God, she shared a name with a goddess—he'd been instantly enchanted. Her silken black hair cascaded down a spine that was ramrod straight, as if her posture had joined forces with her lifted chin to show the world she was impervious, collected, and confident. If the night itself had poured out of a crack in the afternoon sky and formed into a woman, she would be Isis.

He'd had no business with Martin. He needed another horse like he needed a hole in the head. But he couldn't stop himself from going to her. When she turned, those blue eyes seemed to ignite a fire within him. Strange and mysterious, the woman was unusually beautiful. How did one who'd reached maturity and traveled across the ocean maintain unblemished skin with such a healthy vibrance? Then there was her wealth and circumstances. The amount of coin she carried was highly uncommon. A shortage of coin currency in the colonies meant that even the wealthy had resorted to promissory notes. Considering she was an unmarried woman, she must either come from old money or unusual beginnings indeed to carry such a purse.

On the continent, such a thing might not have caught his attention, but here where the population was made up of a concoction of former criminals, military, slaves, clergy, whores, and the occasional scientist such as himself, why would a wealthy family send a daughter to such a place? Isis certainly did not fit the demographic. She was no whore or slave, that was for sure. Her complexion spoke to a Mediterranean heritage, as did her dark hair. Those blue eyes, however, they were the uncommon, deep blue he'd only ever witnessed among northern Europeans. She was a rare beauty, a woman of prime marriageable age. In any other place, she would be wooed by wealthy aristocrats.

Unless she was here because she was running from something. He frowned. Or, like himself, drawn to the promise of discovering something new. Was it possible that Isis Tanglewood was a kindred spirit, an explorer, a scientist?

"Monsieur Baron, we've placed your shipment on the terrace as you requested," his servant Allyette said. The woman was used to strange shipments coming in and out of his home, which she'd nicknamed *Maison de Nuit*, House of Night. Pierre had architected and erected the buildings at the request of the Royal Academy of Sciences, who wished him to conduct research on the natural history of the area. Pierre did run several experiments out of the laboratory within, but it was the two large alcoves built into the second floor he was most excited about. He'd created the first celestial observatory in the colonies, and today, his pursuits were about to experience a major upgrade.

He dismounted his horse and handed the reins to his stableboy before striding inside and up to the second floor. Excitedly, he pried the lid off the crate that waited for him there, brushing aside handfuls of straw packing material. He wondered at the large glass lens that winked at him in the afternoon light. His colleague from England had come through for him with the experimental design. "Monsieur Hall, you've outdone yourself."

Carefully, he removed the pieces from the crate, assembling them with the screws and bolts provided. His heart pounded as the telescope came together. As soon as this night, he'd be able to watch the stars as no one before him had ever done, not from here anyway. Natural history was a noble pursuit, to be sure, but the real advancement of man would surely come from astronomy. Could there be a more important field of study? Already he'd improved naval navigation in this new port city using rudimentary, antiquated tools. This telescope? This could change everything.

He completed the assembly, positioning the telescope atop a wrought-iron tripod he'd had made for the alcove, and focused the lens on the Vieux Carré, being that the sun was far too bright to look at the sky. He made the final adjustments and was delighted with how close everything looked and in such fine detail. Why, he could see a cat on the garden wall as far as the Rue de Bienville on the other end of the square!

Entranced by this, he hardly noticed when Allyette burst in, babbling something about an unexpected guest. "What's that?" Pierre mumbled, his attention completely focused on the telescope.

"Never mind. I'll take it from here," a familiar male voice said.

Pierre removed his eye from the viewer and straightened, muffling a groan. Forcing himself to smile, he pivoted to face Governor Étienne Perier, who loomed in his doorway dressed in his tailored blue jacket and tan breeches. Pierre thought he must be dreadfully hot in the getup, but it was Étienne's way to always appear the height of propriety and discipline, a habit he'd learned as a French naval officer. Étienne was an old friend and part of the reason Pierre enjoyed his position, but his timing couldn't be worse.

"What can I do for you, Governor?" Pierre asked.

"We're alone, my friend. No need for formality. Call me Étienne."

"To what do I owe the pleasure, Étienne?"

He tapped the crate with the toe of his boot. "First, you can describe the purpose of this strange contraption you've assembled." He strode to Pierre's side and grabbed the tube roughly, sending Pierre's heart into a gallop.

"Please, sir, it is a delicate instrument—a telescope, meant to be used to observe the position of the stars."

Étienne scoffed. "For what purpose?"

"To observe and record how their location changes throughout the year."

The other man gave a low and haughty laugh. "And this is a serious scientific pursuit?"

"Surely, as a former navy lieutenant general, you must appreciate the need for accurate maps of the heavens to aid in navigation."

"Yes, yes, of course, but those maps already exist, Pierre. We in la Nouvelle-Orléans have much more pressing and important matters, pursuits that a man with many talents such as your own could contribute to our new parish."

"What pursuits would those be?"

The governor coupled his hands behind his back and paced the terrace, staring out toward the center of town. "I'm here in an official capacity. If we are to enforce the changes necessary to develop la Nouvelle-Orléans from a land of lawless depravity to a place of order and enlightenment, we must continue down the path laid out by our predecessors. As the parish's architect and engineer, I need you to double your efforts toward this cause."

Pierre stifled a groan. Yes, he carried the title, one assigned to him by Étienne to replace a man named Broutin, whom the governor didn't care for. But Pierre never felt particularly called to the job. Étienne reached into his coat and pulled out a bundle of parchment. Unrolling it, he turned so Pierre could see the drawn squares where buildings now stood, as well as the shaded areas where additional dwellings were planned. "See here. Pauger, God rest his soul, had a vision, and Broutin has worked hard to bring it to life, but now you must finish what he started. We need a prison near the *Place d'Armes*, as soon as one can be built. You are the most qualified man to direct its construction. And we can't stop there. Our numbers are growing. The nuns need the new convent, currently awaiting your direction. The mill must be expanded."

"Of course. I'll apply myself to the task by the end of the month." Pierre tried to sound firm but polite.

"I'd prefer you apply yourself to it *immediately*." Étienne folded his arms, mirroring Pierre's stance, and straightened to his full, intimidating height. "I understand you are a man prone to philosophical thinking and most interested in scholarly pursuits, but they will have to wait."

Pierre sighed. "Very well. You shall have your plan for a prison in a matter of days."

The governor nodded and thumped his shoulder. "Excellent. I look forward to seeing what your brilliant mind can assemble."

Pierre said his goodbyes and grimaced at the governor's back. It appeared the telescope would have to wait. He had work to do.

CHAPTER
FOUR

R iding through the woods along the Mississippi, Isis found she could barely stay upright on her horse. Between the heat, the physical exertion of the ride, and her waning magic, she felt bled of her strength. They needed to get the Tanglewood tree in the ground, eat, drink, and rest to regain their vigor. She sagged in the saddle, her eyes drooping to a close before her body jerked awake. When Rhys finally stopped atop a flat stretch of land at the peak of a small, wooded hill, she almost cried out in relief. He dismounted and checked a strip of blue fabric tied around a tree. Isis suspected it marked the boundary of their land.

"This is it," he said. "We're on the southeast point. The river is to the west. We can camp here tonight. Replenish our strength."

Isis forced herself awake. "No. We must keep going and plant the Tanglewood tree tonight." She eyed the tree, which hung limply from Rhys's saddlebag. It had lost a majority of its leaves, and the remainder were a sickly yellow. "I'm not sure she'll make it until tomorrow."

Medea nodded her agreement. "Isis is right. It must be

planted near the center of our property, beside where we will build our house."

"I'm as tired as you, Rhys, but my sisters know our magic. It has to be tonight." Circe rubbed her giant belly. If she were stronger, Isis would have suggested she carry Circe by shadow. She was capable of moving place to place without a horse when she had to. But the fatigue was too much. They'd have to do it the old-fashioned way.

Rhys mounted his steed and rode next to Circe, where he cradled her face in his hands and made her drink water and a tonic he'd made for her. The man was a powerful wizard but an unrivaled genius when it came to herbs and potions. A pang of jealousy shot through Isis. Someday, she hoped to have a man look at her like that.

For some reason, she thought of Pierre then. She rubbed her eyes. Must be tired. Pierre wasn't a wizard and, at best, would be a pleasant dalliance. Handsome as he was, he was an earth-dweller, and the humans here had proven themselves to be small-minded and destructive when it came to anything they didn't understand.

Rhys looked at the map and then started forward again. Isis urged her horse on. It was another thirty minutes before they reached what Rhys claimed was the center of their property. This would be where they built their new home and must be where they planted the tree.

"Sisters?" Medea slid off her horse, looking ten years older than her actual age. She raised her wand and, drawing a symbol in the air, gouged out a section of earth. Rhys helped Circe down and then carried the pitiful-looking Tanglewood tree to the hole and carefully set it inside. Circe packed the dirt around the trunk, frowning at the sagging branches. Shadows gathered around Isis in the twilight as she joined her sisters at the planted tree.

"She's ready," Medea said.

Each of them extended their wrists over the dirt, raised their wands, and slashed. Magic parted Isis's skin, and blood poured onto the roots, splashed leaves, and stained branches. She grunted as her body further weakened from the loss, but she knew it was necessary. They'd never lived without the Tanglewood tree. She had no idea what would happen to them if the tree died, but she never wanted to find out.

"That should be enough," Medea said. They each twirled their wands, and the blood slowed and then stopped.

Circe stumbled, and Rhys caught her in his arms. "Isis, she needs rest."

There was no question why Rhys looked to her specifically at that moment. The sun had set, and her magic was now the strongest of the three, despite her fatigue. She sighed and raised her wand once more. "I've got it."

With an uttered incantation and a flick of her wrist, she made the tent untie itself from the back of her horse, unroll, and lift. Another flick and the canvas stretched, the poles growing to three times their size and staking themselves to the earth. Magic glowed as the roof was raised and the flaps that served as a door folded themselves into position. A lamp ignited inside.

By the time Isis lowered her wand, almost too exhausted to move, a tent big enough for four stood before them, furnished with beds and blankets and glowing warmly from within. Medea wrapped her arm around Isis's shoulders.

"It's done. Good work. Let me help you." Medea guided her inside. With her sister's help, Isis stripped out of her dress and crawled into bed in only her white linen shift.

To the sound of her family's steady breathing, Isis closed her eyes and allowed sleep to wrap her in its loving arms.

ISIS STOOD ON THE EDGE OF A CLIFF, THE ONLY LIGHT THE AMBIENT glow cast from the sea of windowed buildings that populated the city beyond. She wasn't certain where she was but admired the peace and tranquility. It was quiet, the only sound the whisper of shadows, a darkness that spoke to her soul.

She jerked when a thick, muscular arm wrapped around her chest. "Finally," his deep voice said. "You've returned to me."

Whirling, she looked up into the face of the demon who had haunted her nightmares. His eyes glowed red, and two horns protruded from the sides of a twisted, fang-filled face.

"Asmodeus." Isis crossed and uncrossed her arms between them. Her spell thrust the demon away from her, blowing her hair forward and over her shoulders with her effort. She reached for her wand but found it wasn't with her. She wore only her shift, exactly what she'd worn to bed.

"Be gone, demon," she commanded.

"Isis Tanglewood, do you honestly believe you can command me here in my domain? I know what you're thinking. You're wondering if this is a dream, a harmless detour of your mind."

"Is it?"

"A dream, yes. Harmless, no. You're here with me, and what happens here is very much real." His pointed tail flicked behind his obscenely muscled form. "I sense my appearance frightens you. Here, let me fix that." He snapped his taloned fingers, and his body morphed into the image of a devastatingly handsome man in formal wear. He brushed his hands down the sleeves of his waistcoat and straightened the ruffled cuffs of the shirt beneath. His pale blond hair formed a dashing coif, and a straight nose extended over a pearlescent smile.

Lust rolled through her, like warm velvet along the underside of her skin. Her core ached, and her breasts grew heavy, their peaks tightening and straining against the thin linen of her shift. She shook her head, trying to clear it of the demon's overtly sexual power.

"What form you take is no matter," Isis said, swallowing hard against the feelings he evoked in her traitorous body. "I have refused you before, and I will again. I am not yours and never will be."

"You would dare deny me?" the demon crooned. "After what I did for you?"

She raised her chin defiantly. "You did nothing for me."

"What a short memory you have, Isis. I allowed you to take your sister Medea from my realm back to the living." He moved closer to her, his lascivious gaze hot on her skin. "You could not have done it without my assistance."

Isis bared her teeth. "I did that of my own power."

He paced, his gaze raking her body as he circled her. "And I allowed it. I could have stopped you, but I didn't."

She considered arguing that not stopping someone and assisting someone were two different things but decided not to waste her breath. Instead, she asked, "Why didn't you stop me?"

"Because I find you... amusing." His gaze flicked over her again, and he licked his lips.

"Not amusing enough for you to allow Phineas to return with his mother." Isis ground her teeth.

The corners of Asmodeus's mouth turned up. "Ah, the babe. I was wondering when you'd ask me about him." He placed the long, tapered fingers of his right hand to his chest, his blue eyes twinkling as if lit from within. "I cannot take responsibility for the shortcomings of your magic, Isis. You failed to consider the babe when crafting your spell."

It was true. When she'd raised Medea, pregnant with Phineas, from the dead, she hadn't considered how to factor in the baby. She'd never raised anything larger than a sheep before that night. It was her fault that Phineas was still dead. A pit opened in her torso, thinking about her sister's grief. She closed her eyes. Would Medea ever forgive her, truly? How could she, after such a loss?

Asmodeus inhaled and cupped her cheek. "There, there, dear witch. I can offer you a cure for that pesky guilt. Align yourself to me, and I will give you the ultimate power over death. Who knows? With your magic, you might find a way to raise the babe, even now. You might even be able to raise the dragon."

She opened her eyes and looked up into Asmodeus's face. Cloaked in illusion, he was stunningly beautiful, his cool blond appearance elevating him to a work of art, godlike and glowing. But when he smiled, she saw only cruelty in it. A genuine smile could not be constructed out of magic any more than true love could be. The demon had never known either, despite his fervor for lust.

Her body thrummed, her breasts growing heavy and the throb between her legs increasing in its intensity. It was all his doing. She was mortified to catch herself stroking a hand over her own chest and down her stomach, desperate for relief from the aching sensation between her thighs.

"No," she said through her teeth, forcing herself away. "Find someone else. I do not want your power, or the curse that will undoubtedly come with it."

He growled, his smile sprouting fangs as his illusion broke. She gathered her power about her. It was easy here, where shadows ruled. Asmodeus squinted at the tendrils of darkness that wound around her and scowled.

"This is your last chance," he said through his teeth. "Accept my offer and become my lover. Together, we will command the night. You'll be the most powerful witch of your generation."

She forced herself to meet his eyes and shivered. They'd gone black and slitted, like a snake's. "No. I refuse your offer."

"So be it, witch." He morphed back into his red-skinned, horned, and tailed form. "But know this, I will offer you no more favors. Should you enter my realm again, I will be far less amiable." He slashed a hand between them.

Shadows swarmed her, blotting out all light, and carried her away.

She opened her eyes to the sound of birds singing and early morning light streaming through the canvas. Beside her, her sisters and Rhys slept peacefully. Her gaze fell on Medea, and the heaviness returned to her chest. Goddess, she didn't regret resurrecting her sister. She couldn't. But she might never recover from the guilt. The pain on her sister's face when she'd learned that she'd lost both her mate and her unborn child had been almost too much to bear. Phineas and Tavyss were gone. Nothing could be done about it but to carry the burden of her choice.

On bare feet, she padded out the tent flap to take a deep breath of fresh morning air. When her eyes fell on the Tanglewood tree, she could not hold back her elation. She raised her hands to her mouth and simply allowed the joy to sweep every dark thought she'd had away.

"It worked! Sisters, it worked!" she cried.

What last night was a sapling struggling to cling to its last shred of life, was now at least ten feet tall, its braided trunk solid and strong. She walked under its lush branches and placed her hands on the section that was smooth and sleek, just like her wand, with elongated knots that stretched toward the sun. The branches that grew from it were home to darker green leaves than the rest of the tree. They wrapped low around the trunk, preferring the shade from Medea's and Circe's branches.

"Good to have you back, my friend," she said to the tree, placing a kiss upon its bark.

A scuffle behind her announced Circe and Medea at the tent flap. Their faces lit up just as hers had, and they rushed to her side.

"It worked!" Circe squealed, rounding the tree to the part that birthed her wand. Its trunk veered toward the center of the tree and went straight up, exploding into tiny, pale leaves that danced in the slightest breeze.

Medea leaned into the side of the tree that connected to her magic. It filled in the gaps, blending the energy of Circe's bright magic with Isis's shadowy sorcery. "Oh, I can feel it." She rested her forehead against the bark. "Thank the goddess."

Rhys ran a hand through his beard. "Incredible. It's like we never uprooted her."

"If anything, I feel stronger than before," Circe said. "I think she likes it here."

After a few moments appreciating the tree's beauty, Medea grew restless and turned to face the wooded horizon. "Come, sisters. It's time to build our future."

DAYS LATER, ISIS STOOD ON THE WRAPAROUND PORCH OF THE BIG farmhouse, staring out across a field of indigo that was just sprouting from the fertile soil. They'd constructed the house using magic, felling the trees, slicing them into boards and interlocking them in the way that homes were built in Darnuith. It felt like home, made more so by the furnishings they'd conjured or brought with them from France.

"Finally, a place to lay roots," Circe said. Rhys took her hands and started dancing with her to a song that must have been in both of their heads because they moved in perfect unison beside her.

Medea smiled warmly. "Brings back memories." Tears welled in her eyes.

As much as Isis wanted to be happy for Circe, her chest felt heavy as if a ball of lead had formed there. She'd never been in love. Never felt the all-encompassing need for another person the way Rhys and Circe seemed to feel about each other. There was ownership there, as if they were two parts of a whole that had finally found each other, completing each other. Medea had it with Tavyss before he was killed and Circe had it with Rhys now, but Isis had never experienced it. And although she was delighted for both her sisters, she felt an acute emptiness at the thought.

If she could never trust anyone here with who she really was...what she really was...she'd never love or be loved. What kind of life, then, would remain for her? Was she to exist as no more than an accessory to her sister's relationship? A sidekick to Circe's story?

Tears pricked her eyes. It wasn't enough. She wanted more.

"Sister, is everything all right?" Medea asked.

Isis blinked away her unshed tears. "Excuse me. I need some rest."

She climbed the winding staircase at the center of the house and entered the room she'd chosen as her own. It was sparsely decorated with a four-poster bed and a set of drawers. But it was the full-length mirror in the corner she sought out. Wiping under her eyes, she opened the wooden box she kept on her dresser and retrieved a single hair, the color of coffee grounds.

She shouldn't use it.

Nothing could ever happen between her and Pierre.

Just one look couldn't hurt, though, could it?

Raising her wand, she pressed the hair against the silver and muttered a spell. The hair sank into the mirror, the surface rippling like a disturbed pool. And there he was.

CHAPTER
FIVE

Pierre sketched the blooms of the oleander tree into his journal, anxious to write to his colleague in France about the plant's properties. The parish's new botanical garden was coming together nicely, with a growing selection of native plants, now named, hazards and uses identified. Eventually, he planned to publish his findings in a guidebook of the region.

"What stunning pink flowers." Her voice came from behind him just as the scent of evening primrose and something fresh—cucumber, he decided—met his nose.

He stood and whirled, finding her smiling under the shade of a parasol. "Isis, what a pleasure to see you again." It *was* an intense pleasure. The woman was as stunningly beautiful as he remembered.

Her smile grew wider. "And you, Pierre." She approached, grazing his shoulder with her own as she gazed down at his notebook. "Is this the secret occupation you refused to share with me days ago? You study plants?"

Pierre cleared his throat, but his tongue felt thick as he spoke. "One of them."

Her brows rose toward expertly coiffed black hair. "A man of many talents."

"I prefer to think of myself as a student of many disciplines," he said. "What is science after all, but an organized desire to know things previously unknown?"

"Ah, another clue. You are a scientist."

He shot her a flirtatious smile. "I'm onto you, Isis. You're trying to guess my secret without giving me the honor of accepting my invitation for tea."

"It's true, I haven't accepted, *yet*. But I also haven't turned down the invitation."

"A woman who likes to keep her options open."

"Always." She glanced again at his unfinished drawing. "Please don't stop on my account."

He turned and sat on the large rock behind him, gesturing for her to do the same. He dusted the boulder with his hand. "I have no jacket to spread for you."

"Good. It's far too hot for one, and I have no fear of a little dust." She sat down beside him. "Tell me about this plant."

He slanted her a wry grin. "Oleander. Interestingly enough, this plant is a lot like a woman. As you can see, the delicate pink blooms are a delight to behold. But she harbors a secret. A single petal is toxic enough to kill a man. Beautiful but deadly. Nature's lethal combination."

Isis laughed. "You think women are deadly?"

"Maybe not in the sense of swords and pistols, but your sex doles out ample quantities of sweet poison capable of wrenching a man's heart from his chest with a single kiss."

"Historically, I believe swords and pistols have been far more effective."

"What of Helen of Troy?"

"What of Anne Boleyn?"

His gaze locked with hers. He'd known she was beautiful, but her quick wit was equally as intoxicating. "It's settled, then. Men and women are each other's undoing, equally and as lethally toxic as this plant." He pointed a hand at the oleander.

"Oh, I don't know. It seems some couplings heal rather than kill. I was born and raised in a garden, not unlike this one, and my parents were nothing if not medicine for each other. They knew nothing but happiness."

"A rare combination, then."

"Maybe it all comes down to the dose." She stood. "I should go, before my company starts to taste bitter."

"*Non*, I haven't had nearly enough of your poison." He grabbed her wrist playfully. Their eyes locked again, and it was as if he'd captured lightning in a jar. A shock ran up his arm, and his entire body tingled with the need to touch more of her, to taste her.

Slowly, she pulled her arm from his grip. "Another time." She curtsied and then moved down the path toward the entrance to the garden.

He looked back at the oleander tree, thinking he should be content to let her go. Then he thought better of it. He'd ask to court her, find out where she lived, and make a habit of stopping by. He popped off his rock and raced after her, but Isis was gone.

It was another three days before he saw her again. This time, he'd left the site where he was overseeing the construction of the new convent and found a shady, moss-covered spot to rest, just beyond the limits of the Vieux Carré, when she appeared with a picnic basket on her arm.

"Isis Tanglewood, what in heaven's name are you doing here?"

She grinned. "Investigating. It seems I've discovered another of your talents." She looked over her shoulder, in the direction of the convent. "You build things."

"I design buildings," he corrected. "It's not I who wields the hammer."

"An architect and a scientist. There. I know all your secrets." She was wearing a green dress today, and before he could say another word, she spread a blanket beside him and dug into the basket. He hadn't eaten anything since early that morning, and he accepted the plate she made for him with genuine gratitude.

"Do you make it a habit of trolling the street with picnic baskets for any man lucky enough to catch your attention?"

"Oh, I packed this one especially for you."

His heart did a jig at the thought. "How did you know where I would be?"

The corner of her mouth lifted. "I'm incredibly resourceful."

"You came here specifically for me?" he asked softly.

She gave a single nod.

"I'm honored," he said. "I find you occupy my thoughts rather persistently as of late."

With her legs stretched out in front of her, she smoothed her skirt over her knees. "I'm sure you have many things to occupy your thoughts."

"Oh, I do. For example, I was just thinking how appropriate it was that your parents named you Isis. She was an Egyptian goddess who legend says could create or destroy life with a single word."

Isis leaned back on her elbows and stared up at the sky. "And how is that like me?"

Pierre ate a piece of apple from his plate. "You could create or destroy me with a single word. Saying yes to courting me would certainly bring me to life."

Her gaze shifted to his, and the smile faded from her face. "The things you say. I'm sure a botanist and architect such as yourself has many women clamoring for your company."

"But only one who has my full and undivided attention." God, the way she was looking at him. It was clear she was as affected by his presence as he was hers. He wondered why she was playing coy.

For a few long moments, they ate in silence as Isis seemed to consider his words. "I find myself drawn to you, Pierre, in a way I haven't experienced before. But..."

"Yes."

She lifted her eyes to his. "You are not the only one with secrets," she whispered.

His lips twitched. "You forget, I'm a scientist. I love a good mystery. Whatever it is, Isis, the stranger the situation, the more intrigued I will be." He laughed. He'd known from their first meeting that she had secrets. The money...her beauty...the strange circumstances of her family. Growing up in a garden was also a clue. Thinking about it now, he hypothesized that she was the daughter of pirates, likely raised on an island and wealthy by unlawful means. He didn't mind. Pierre had never been the self-righteous sort, and her parents' sins were hardly her own.

"I should be going." She finished what was on her plate and started gathering things into the basket.

"You haven't learned all my secrets, you know. You haven't even discovered my primary occupation."

She paused. "There's something else?"

39

He gave her a formal nod. "There is. Something I can only show you at my home at night."

She burst into laughter. "Now it has to be at night?"

He shrugged. "I have no control over this aspect. You must come and see for yourself. Find a chaperone of your choosing, come to my home, and I will show you my true passion. Or, better yet, tell me where you live, and I will court you properly."

She packed up the rest of the picnic, including his empty plate, and stood. "As always, you've given me plenty to think about, Pierre."

"When will I see you again?" he asked.

"When I can't stay away," she said far too seriously. She started to leave, and Pierre scrambled to his feet, hoping to walk her home. He'd only glanced away for a moment to brush himself off, but when he looked in her direction again, she was gone. Completely gone. And he was left wondering what kind of secrets Isis Tanglewood was harboring.

CHAPTER
SIX

Days passed, and Isis felt herself become more and more restless. She'd thought visiting with Pierre would help get him out of her system, but the more she learned about the man, the more drawn she was to him. There was something about the way he looked at her, like she was a jewel and he was studying her every facet, entranced by her color and depth. Pierre had said she had his undivided attention, and she knew it was true. The intensity he focused on her was unmatched.

Which was why she'd stayed away. He was too much of a temptation. Already, she desperately wished to know him and to be known by him. But she was a witch, and he was an earth-dweller. She'd already risked too much, meeting him the way she had.

"Isis, by the goddess, you're going to wear a path into the floor. What has gotten into you?" Medea asked.

"I think I need some exercise. I'm going to go exploring." She headed for the back door.

"Be careful, sister. These lands harbor beasts unknown."

Drawing her wand, she grinned and called the shadows to her, tongues of darkness spiraling to her will like a den of angry vipers. "Then it's time they met their fiercest neighbor."

She allowed the blackness to swallow her and carry her into the nearby forest. She'd wanted to be alone, but her solitude among the oaks and cypress trees was far from silent. Birds sang, insects buzzed, and the grunts of wild boars filled the space around her. For some reason, she thought of Pierre then. Did he know things about boars like he did about horses and plants and building things?

Her kind didn't "court" the way earth-dwellers did, but if they'd been in Darnuith and Pierre were a wizard, she would have gone out with him enthusiastically. Yes, she would have enjoyed that. He interested her, and his presence evoked an intense and immediate attraction she'd never experienced before.

But her sisters would never allow it here. Medea had made it perfectly clear that their greatest priority was discretion. They couldn't trust these people, and Isis was well aware that what she'd done for Medea, bringing her back from the dead, she could never do again. They could not afford to risk attracting the wrong kind of attention here. She knew this, but still, she grieved for herself, for the experiences she sensed she was missing, for what might have been.

Up ahead, through the moss-draped cypress trees, a swamp came into view. She was in the farthest corner of their property, a place they hadn't spent much time yet. An alligator wound its way across the murky depths. She approached the bank, fascinated by the creature's graceful movements, her wand gripped in her hand, ready to transport her out of harm's way should the creature attack.

She was still watching the six-foot-long reptile when the base of her neck started to tingle and she caught a whiff of sulfur on the air. Death. She sensed it nearby as certainly as if she were in the underworld.

Isis spun, searching for the source, as shadows stirred around her, roused by her sudden apprehension. She could find nothing unusual about the swamp. Nothing dead in the area around her. But still, the magic inside her continued on high alert. What was she missing?

Tingling with apprehension, she tipped her head back and looked straight up. What she saw in the tree above her sent her leaping back, clutching her chest. A dead man, blanched white as if he'd been drained of blood, draped over a branch above her head. His pallid arms dangled toward her. Isis couldn't see his face, but that forearm was eerily familiar, and it was branded with the fleur-de-lis.

CHAPTER
SEVEN

P ierre strode into the governor's office with a roll of parchment under his arm. On it was his updated architectural drawing for a new prison. To be sure, Pierre knew nothing about prisons and had never had any desire to direct the building of one, but this was the job Étienne needed him to do, and he'd agreed to do it.

The governor's private home neighbored his own, but Étienne did business out of a well-proportioned administrative barracks two blocks west. The door had been propped open to allow a breeze to pass through the place and out the back windows. It was a shady respite from the sweltering heat, and Pierre hurried inside. He stopped short when he noticed the governor was not alone.

"Ah, Monsieur Baron, have you met Madame Delphine Laurent?" The governor pointed a hand at the woman sitting in the chair across the desk from him. "Madame, this is Pierre Baron, engineer and architect of the parish."

"Laurent still seems strange to my ears. It's been only days since I went by Devereaux." Delphine blotted her eyes with a handkerchief and turned to face Pierre. Her hair, shiny and a deep, rich brown, almost black, was curled and piled atop her head in a style the women of the area often saved for more formal occasions. Her skin was milky white and silky smooth, unusual for this part of the world. He'd never met her before, which meant she must have arrived recently. He immediately wondered if she'd met Isis.

Pierre bowed at the waist. "*Enchante*, Madame Laurent, and congratulations on your recent marriage. I hope I have not interrupted."

She dabbed her handkerchief in the corner of each eye, although Pierre didn't notice any tears necessitating the motion. Her powder seemed to be firmly in place as she said, "Oh, but I'm afraid you have. You see, my husband has gone missing. He didn't come home last night. I fear the worst."

Étienne sighed. "I was just explaining to Delphine that the, er, culture here is different from in France, and many new husbands spend time away from their wives until they become accustomed to the marital relationship." The governor coughed into his hand as if the lie burned his throat.

The truth was that this parish was a den of debauchery and that her husband had likely spent the night drinking and whoring and would return to her when he got hungry for a home-cooked meal or needed a sock mended. A good number of men in la Nouvelle-Orléans were former prisoners, hardened and depraved. If Pierre's memory served, Monsieur Laurent was just such a man.

Immediately, his heart went out to the woman, but then he noticed something...odd. Although her expression was grim, Pierre couldn't help but observe that her spine remained straight, her shoulders back as if to try to make the most of her figure in the lightweight dress she wore.

And her frown, though pronounced, had not dulled the light in her bright amber eyes. Such an unusual pale shade of brown, those eyes, almost yellow. Her grief had not dulled her beauty in the slightest. Then again, could he expect that a woman who had wed only days ago would be any more distraught over a missing husband—a man who was, for all intents and purposes, a stranger?

Pierre gave her a sympathetic look. "I am sure, wherever your husband is, he regrets not being in the company of such a lovely bride."

A shallow smile graced her lips, and her gaze sought out his. "I see now how you came to be in your position, Monsieur Baron. You have quite the imagination."

They were interrupted when a young man in uniform rushed in, face pale and hands trembling. "Sir, you must come. There's a... A man was found in the river. A dead man."

After a quick exchange of glances, Pierre accompanied the governor, as did Madame Laurent, into a waiting carriage that took them to the bank of the Mississippi. Pierre wondered at the wisdom of bringing Delphine along. If the man was her missing husband, would she dissolve into hysterics? But across from him, Delphine seemed utterly cool and collected. She didn't sweat, he observed, although the carriage was quite hot. Now that he studied her, he found her almost statuesque in appearance and wondered if the day's events had stunned her into the stony expression. She hadn't even blinked in several seconds.

He was relieved when they arrived, and she stepped gracefully down from her seat, even if her face did retain its impassive expression. He fixed his eyes on the crowd that had gathered near the river. Why should he feel the need to examine Madame Laurent? Surely there was no common way of reacting to such events.

Pierre halted his line of thinking altogether when he saw the body washed upon the shore. The surgeon and coroner, Alexandre Viel, was already there, frowning and shaking his head. When he saw the governor, he approached them, sparing a curt nod for Delphine.

"Washed up this morning," Viel said. "We're having trouble identifying him. The body has been completely drained of blood."

Delphine strode forward, the hem of her pale gray dress sweeping the rocky shore. Viel and the young soldier called out warnings, insisting that she not approach the body, but she did so anyway. To Pierre's astonishment, she dug the toe of her shoe into the corpse's shoulder and rolled the body over, until the bloated face stared up at her.

Pierre raised a hand to his mouth, surprised that Delphine had no reaction to the ghastly sight near her feet. The dead man's neck sported two puncture wounds as if he'd been bitten by a massive snake, and his skin adhered tightly to the bones.

"It is my husband," Delphine said coolly, then pressed her handkerchief to the corner of her eye again. "This is Guillaume Laurent."

She turned on her heel and strode back toward the carriage with her handkerchief held to her face. Pierre took another look at the dead man. His arm had flopped to the side when Delphine had rolled him over, and a fleur-de-lis tattoo marred his forearm. A former prisoner, then. Pierre wondered what kind of trouble the man had got himself into.

"What animal drains a body of its blood but leaves the flesh?" Étienne frowned. "Unless Viel shows me evidence the man was attacked by a swarm of leeches following such a bite, I suspect Guillaume was murdered before being thrown into the river."

"But who would murder a man in such a strange way? And why?" Pierre asked.

Étienne's gray eyes turned hard as ice. "Most certainly the Indians. We've had issues with them resisting the civilization we bring here. I think the savages are sending us a message."

"What do you plan to do?"

"What can be done except to kill or cage the offenders?"

Forcing his eyes away, Pierre made for the carriage. "Then let us discuss your prison so that when you find this murderer, you'll be ready."

"I KEEP THINKING ABOUT WHAT WE DID," ISIS SAID TO MEDEA as they sipped their tea in the front room of the big house. "Shouldn't we have told someone? Or left the dead man in town for the authorities to find?"

Once they'd used magic to get the dead body out of the tree, they'd identified him as the stranger who'd pulled the knife in the crowd when they'd disembarked in la Nouvelle-Orléans. They'd quickly determined the cause of his death and, after a short discussion, gave him a burial at sea of sorts, floating him down the Mississippi, off their property and beyond their realm of responsibility.

"He'd been drained by a vampire," Medea said. "We can't risk being associated with magical creatures. This way, someone else will find the dead man, somewhere far from us."

"I wasn't aware vampires existed in this world. I haven't

seen one since Ouros." Until the body, Isis had been under the impression that she, Rhys, and her sisters were the only magical creatures in this realm.

"If one is among us, it will likely kill again," Medea said. "We are strangers here. It would be too easy for someone to accuse us if its victims are found on our property. After tea, I'll ward the property against them."

Isis nodded. Warding the property was a good idea for a number of reasons, but Medea was underestimating the citizens of this parish if she thought that would be enough. "Even if the killings do not occur near us, people are bound to notice a pattern among the dead and missing. Whether the colonists are aware of vampires or not, this could come back to haunt us. What will they think if we seem immune to the terrifying deaths that are about to descend here?"

Medea grunted her displeasure. "You're right, sister. This vampire is a risk to us all. At worst, we might be blamed for its victims. At best, its continued feeding in this area might make the colonists hypervigilant against anything perceived to be supernatural, also a risk to us."

"We need to find this vampire and try to convince it to leave *la Nouvelle-Orléans*," Isis said.

"How do you suppose we do that? Vampires are apex predators. One will not take kindly to our request, even if we are lucky enough to find the creature."

"True. It's almost impossible to find a vampire who doesn't want to be found, but it's not impossible to draw them out. If I go into town tonight, I might be able to use the shadows to ignite its curiosity."

"I don't like it. A woman alone at night in this part of the world will most certainly attract scrutiny. You may draw out the vampire, but you also risk garnering the suspicion of the locals."

Isis thought for a moment. "The man who helped me buy the horses showed interest in me," she said plainly. "Not as a witch, but as a woman. I think I can use that as an excuse to be there. He might even have answers to our questions about how much the colonists know about the creatures and if this has ever happened before."

The corner of Medea's mouth twitched. "Truly? And you don't mind leveraging his attraction to you for information?"

"No, I don't mind." Isis was proud of how measured the words came out. Inside, she was anxious to have a reason to see Pierre again, although she'd never admit her ulterior motives to Medea. This was her chance, with Medea's blessing, no less!

"Do you know where he lives or how to find him again?"

"Yes. I can go this evening."

Medea sipped her tea. "Very well. But be careful, Isis. The women here do not share the freedoms we are accustomed to. Your idea is a good one, and hopefully this man you speak of will respond positively to your visit, as will the vampire, if you can flush it out. But if things go wrong—"

"I'll have the shadows to protect me. I promise I'll make use of them if I need to."

"Good." Medea darted a glance in her direction. "If you're not back by midnight, I'll come looking for you."

Isis stood and placed her empty cup on the tray. "It's settled, then. I'll leave at twilight."

51

"I CAN DO IT, BUT I DON'T KNOW WHAT STYLES ARE POPULAR here," Circe said, raising her wand and pointing it at Isis's Caribbean-style linen dress.

"Make it silk and lace," Isis said, picturing it in her mind. "Blue and black. Like the ones in Paris in the summer."

Circe sighed. "Are you sure? I didn't see a shred of silk when we were in town."

"We only recently arrived. No one will question it."

With a shrug, Circe cast her enchantment at Isis's apparel. The fabric fluttered as if it had come alive, then sparked with magic. The shimmer grew brighter, power billowing the skirt from her body and transforming her dress from her shoulders down. Once the spell had run its course, it sank into the earth, and Isis swayed, appreciating the results. The royal-blue silk shimmered. A square of black lace wrapped around the back of her neck and tucked into her plunging neckline, while matching lace edged the sleeves at her elbows. The bodice was tight, but the skirt flared over her black heeled boots. She patted the small hat that secured her hair in place.

"It's lovely. It brings out your eyes," Circe said. "I suspect you'll steal Pierre's breath."

"She's not going there to steal anyone's breath. She's going to bait a vampire into revealing itself," Medea insisted.

Circe waved a hand dismissively. "She can do both, Medea. Let a girl have some fun."

Isis mounted her horse, adjusting her skirt around her legs. The dress wasn't meant for riding, but with a little magic, it would do. "Anyway, I need Pierre to have his breath so he can answer my questions."

"Oh, I think he'll take one look at you and give you

whatever you need," Circe said.

Medea scowled.

"Then I'm off." She waved to her sisters and Rhys and called the shadows to her. Oh, she could ride into town, but traveling by shadow would be faster. She leaned down closer to her horse's neck. Darkness swirled around her, blocking out the moon, and then she was deposited on the edge of the Vieux Carré. Her horse snorted and bobbed its head at the sudden change in scenery. "You're all right, Sunset." She patted the horse's neck. "Come on. Let us find this tavern Pierre mentioned."

She urged the horse forward to the town square and followed the sound of laughter to Touze's, a small but lively tavern on *Rue de Bourbon*. She dismounted and strode inside, straight up to the bar. Raucous voices seemed to quiet upon her arrival, and heads turned to look at her.

"Can I help you, *mademoiselle*?" the barkeep asked.

"Is Monsieur Touze here?" she asked.

"That would be me." The man tugged on the gray hair of his beard. "It must be my lucky day to be called on by such a beautiful woman."

Isis ignored the compliment and jumped straight to the point. "I'm looking for Pierre Baron. He said you would know where to find him."

He let loose a crooked smile, "You're in luck." Touze yelled toward his back room. "Pierre, there's someone here to see you!"

Monsieur Baron appeared at the end of the bar, his sleeves rolled past his elbows. As always, he was a vision of masculine strength, dark and intense, with a body forged in the wilds of Louisiana. For a moment, she forgot why she was there and simply appreciated the view. He did a double take. "Isis?"

"You said to come at night." She sent him her most disarming smile.

He approached her and lowered his voice. "Are you here alone?"

"I am," she said, noticing then that she was one of only three women in the place, and the other two seemed completely devoted to entertaining the gentlemen in their company.

He exchanged a few words with Nicholas. "Come with me."

She hooked her arm into his and they started for the door, but she stopped short when her eyes caught on another woman at the back of the crowded room. *Delphine Devereaux*. But oh, how she'd changed since their last encounter. Gone was the sickly, pale woman Isis had met with the cough and blood-stained lips, replaced by a bright-eyed, smooth-skinned creature with healthy curves. *Vampire*, Isis thought, but it was impossible. She didn't know for sure how vampires in Ouros became vampires except that they were not previously human.

Delphine sent her a tight-lipped smile that oozed menace.

"What is it?" Pierre asked, darting a glance over his shoulder in the direction she'd been looking.

Isis glanced at him and then back toward Delphine, but she was gone. A chill coursed through her. "I thought I saw a woman I met on the ship from Paris. Her name was Delphine Devereaux. Do you know her?"

Pierre sighed. "Delphine Laurent now, by marriage, although I'm sad to say her circumstances are such that I doubt it was her you saw."

"Oh?"

"She wouldn't be here. Lost her husband only today, I'm afraid. Last I heard, she was consumed with grief."

Isis scanned the crowd again for the woman, but she had truly disappeared. "How horrifying for her to lose a husband when she was so recently married." *To a vampire,* she added in her head.

"Terrible tragedy."

How to ask what she needed to... what she suspected. "Was her husband advanced in years?"

Pierre snorted. "Afraid not." He tugged on her arm, leading her outside. "Tragic circumstances. Best not discuss them here." He gestured toward a horse and wagon nearby, the bed filled with oak kegs. "Care to ride with me? My home isn't far, but it's not safe to walk this time of night."

"Strangely enough, I've always felt safer at night," she said, intentionally baiting him to tell her what dangers he believed the night possessed. In fact, Isis was sure she was the most dangerous thing in all of la Nouvelle-Orléans. Even now, the shadows caressed her ankles, waiting to serve her. But she needed Pierre to tell her if he knew about vampires and to fill in the gaps about Delphine.

He sighed, growing serious. "Perhaps in the French countryside. But here, in the wilds, the darkness is far more dangerous."

"I doubt an alligator will reach me this far from the water."

His gaze traced along the length of her neck. "Alligators are not what concerns me. Isis, you must know what a rare beauty you are. The men here are as wild and untamed as the land. Hasn't anyone warned you about traveling unchaperoned?"

Heat traveled along her neck at the way he looked at her. She'd seen that intensity before between men and women, just never directed at her. "You flatter me, Pierre, and I will take it under advisement. I'm new here, and it appears I've underestimated the risk."

He bowed his head. "In any case, for tonight, you needn't worry. You're safe with me."

Just as she planned. Shadows rose within her, and before she could check herself, she looked at him through her lashes and whispered, "I hope not overly safe. A little danger can be exciting, don't you think?"

He let out a soft grunt, his throat bobbing on a swallow, and offered her his hand. A predatory glint replaced the smile in his eyes. "Leave it to me. I know ways to make your heart race that won't cause you any pain."

A tingle traveled through her, his nearness causing her heart to gallop. The ways he alluded to were no mystery. All he had to do was look at her with that intense gray stare and her pulse pounded in her veins. Without even thinking, she placed her hand in his, but when he attempted to help her onto the bench of his wagon, she balked.

"Oh, I have a horse," she said, gesturing to where Sunset was secured to a post. "I'll follow you."

Only minutes later, she found herself riding toward the gate of a home on the corner of Dumaine and Chartres Streets near the heart of the Vieux Carré. Over the wall, Isis made out a house, two stories tall, with open-air alcoves on the second floor. Something glinted in those inlets of darkness, and she was immediately curious about the architecture and what it might be used for.

"What is it exactly that you do, Monsieur Baron?" she whispered under her breath. He was too far away to hear her. He'd hopped down to unlock and open the massive gate before reseating himself and driving the wagon inside. She followed.

A boy came running from a smaller building which she now understood was a stable. He helped her off her horse.

"Take the horses to the stables, Henri, but remain on hand."

"*Oui, monsieur.*" The boy led Sunset toward the stable.

Isis forced herself to focus on the task that had brought her there. She needed to know more about Delphine and her husband. "Now that we're alone...you were saying about Monsieur Laurent?"

He strode toward the house, gesturing for her to follow. "When I said this place was dangerous, unfortunately I was speaking from direct observation. Guillaume Laurent was found dead this afternoon. His cause of death is unknown, but he was completely drained of blood."

Ice formed in her belly. She'd suspected this, given Delphine's earlier strange appearance, but hearing it still filled her with apprehension. She hadn't known which man had won Delphine as his wife. Now she understood the man with the fleur-de-lis tattoo was Guillaume Laurent, Delphine's husband—Delphine, whom she'd just seen at the tavern looking far too well for someone who was coughing up blood only weeks ago. Guillaume, a victim of a vampire, the man she'd found dead in a tree on her property. As impossible as it seemed, Delphine was almost surely the creature she was after.

Her discomfort must have shown on her face because Pierre placed a hand on her elbow. "I'm sorry if I've unsettled you. I was shocked as well to learn of the strange state of the body. Please, come in. It's not good to discuss the dead in the open."

Isis followed Pierre into a stunning structure, perhaps austere in its décor but avant-garde in design. Compared to the other buildings in the settlement, this one was light and airy, with large, open rooms and high ceilings. She stopped in the entryway to appreciate it as he closed the door behind her.

"When... I mean... How was the body found?"

"Today, on the banks of the Mississippi. Delphine was distraught. She'd been looking for him."

He pointed toward a flight of stairs.

"Delphine was there? In the daylight?" The strange look Pierre shot her prompted her to restate her question. "What I mean is, did the poor woman see the state of the body?"

"I'm afraid so. In the full light of day. There was no hiding the horror of it."

Goddess, that ruled out Delphine being the vampire. It didn't make sense, though. Everything else fit. Unless vampires here were a different sort of creature than in Ouros. How could she get Pierre to tell her more?

"You said Guillaume was drained of his blood," she began. "What or who would do such a thing?"

Both horror and curiosity flitted through his expression. "That's just it. No one knows. Governor Perier suspects the Indians. They've been violent on occasion as our parish expands into their territory. It might have been meant as a warning. But I have other suspicions. Truthfully, Guillaume was not well-liked by many here. Any number of men might have inflicted such a death. I've heard he was overly rough with his slaves. Perhaps one found opportunity for revenge. Or an acquaintance might be to blame. Many of the inhabitants here are former prisoners. Foul play isn't unheard of."

"But you're sure it was a *who* and not a *what*?" she asked. "Could it not have been done by some unknown creature native to the area?"

He grunted. "I'd considered a snake. It looked like a snake bite. But snakes don't generally drink blood."

There was more Isis needed to know, but she had to approach this delicately. He might react in a number of ways to what she was about to say. "I've heard stories in France about a creature called a *vampire* that drains the blood of men. The church says they are people who've been possessed by demons."

Pierre laughed. "Scary stories to frighten children who won't obey. Vampires don't truly exist."

Interesting. So the people here didn't believe in vampires. But they most certainly believed in and feared witches. Medea was right; Isis and her sisters needed to be very careful, because one slip and they would likely be blamed for the vampire's victims.

They'd reached the second floor and the end of the hallway, where a door waited. Pierre opened it for her, and cool night air wafted over her. It might as well have been a portal to another world. She was standing on one of the terraces she'd seen from below, looking out over the parish, a star-studded night sky above her. At the center of the alcove, a contraption stood. She recognized what it was immediately. She'd used something similar in Darnuith.

"You own a telescope!" She gasped in wonder. "This is an observatory."

A twinkle of excitement danced in his eyes. "Two, actually. Are you familiar with their use?"

"*Oui.*" When he seemed surprised, she added, "There was an observatory where I am from."

He looked utterly confused. "I was not aware of any astronomers in the region of Provence, and I am a member of the Royal Academy of Sciences."

She chastised herself internally. Why had she admitted

knowing how to use the machine? When would she learn that many things in Darnuith did not exist here? Technology she'd taken for granted was in its infancy here.

"It was a private endeavor by a wealthy businessman," she explained quickly. "I would hardly call its use scientific." She hoped he'd buy the explanation.

He seemed to because he adjusted the viewer and gestured to it. She peered through the lens and gasped. Goddess, the glory of it. The stars seemed to go on forever, and through the telescope, the Earth's singular moon looked close enough to reach out and touch.

"This," he said formally, "is what I do."

She turned her face from the viewer. "You chart the stars?"

"And more. Only two years ago, I observed a total lunar eclipse and, earlier this year, the emergence of Jupiter's moon. I believe I can use the observations to improve the accuracy of our maps and pinpoint the location of la Nouvelle-Orléans in relation to Paris." The topic seemed to ignite a fire within him until he glowed with boyish exuberance.

She smiled softly. "I think your passion for the heavens is contagious."

He moved closer, his hand lifting to touch the viewer. She didn't move away, and his fingers brushed hers. The scent of him, like sawdust, whiskey, and virile male. Her pulse reacted, and the shadows slithered around her ankles. What would it feel like to kiss him? She'd only kissed one man before, Brody, a friend in Darnuith whose lips ignited nothing within her when they touched her own. How different it would be with Pierre, who'd enchanted her without any magic at all.

"With a name like Isis, I'd be surprised if you weren't

passionate about the heavens long before me." He fixated on her mouth. "I never asked, how did you come by such a name?"

Isis remembered the lie she'd told Delphine, but for some reason, she couldn't bring herself to lie to Pierre. "My parents believed the goddess helped them survive a difficult time in their lives."

"Fascinating. I studied her in university. She's a compelling mythological character."

She grinned. *Mythology*. If he only knew how very real Isis actually was.

"I wish now I'd spent more time studying astronomy, but the truth is, I've never had the fervor you seem to about the stars. Certainly, I appreciate their beauty, but they are so far beyond our reach. It's not as if they hold answers to life's deepest questions."

"Don't they?" He stood back a step and lifted his chin, taking in the fullness of the night sky. "Aren't we told that we are bound for the heavens when we die?"

Isis gave a light laugh.

"You do believe in heaven, don't you?"

She schooled her features and cleared her throat. There was an afterlife. She'd seen it—well, not precisely the final destination in the journey, but the stepping-off point. How to say it, though, in a way that would suit his mind. "I do believe in heaven." She nodded. "But I don't believe it's there." She pointed at the stars.

"Then where?" His voice was quiet now, and she heard old grief weighing down its volume. Pierre had lost someone, and this question was personal. "Where does death take us when we die?"

She placed her hand on his arm. "It's another realm.

Another...reality, as real as our own but not accessible by us in this form."

"You say it with such certainty."

"Because I am sure." What was she doing? She was circling much too closely to the truth right now. "Only because I've experienced loss and followed death in my dreams."

He turned to her then, his hand coming to rest on top of her own. His eyes were the most arresting shade of gray, like polished steel. "I know that feeling. I lost my father only five years ago." He breathed a deep sigh. "That's it, then."

"Hmm?"

"Why I'm so incredibly drawn to you. We have something in common—a connection. A loss...a past grief... Who was yours?"

"My nephew," she said, before she had a chance to second-guess herself. "As a baby."

"I'm sorry for your loss."

They stood in companionable silence for a moment, Isis staring up at the stars. When she looked back at Pierre to ask him to teach her about the constellations, their eyes locked, his suddenly gleaming like a predator's. He stepped closer to her, and she raised her hands to rest them on his chest. Nothing but hard, lean muscle existed under his shirt. His gaze fixated on her mouth, their nearness infusing the air with tension. One of her shadows tousled his hair, and she shooed it away with her will. He leaned in closer. So... close... Was this a dream? Some type of magic was at work, considering the way her body ached for him.

Everything else fell away as he touched his lips to hers.

CHAPTER
EIGHT

Pierre considered himself a gentleman and a man of science. He'd never hired a prostitute or brought strange women to his bed. He'd taken lovers over the years but always women he knew well and who consented to the arrangement. When those relationships ended, because the woman took a husband or became enthralled with someone else, he parted ways amicably. In short, he was a disciplined man who'd never accomplished divorcing physical pleasures from emotional ones.

As he pulled Isis into his arms, surprise heightened his senses and made the entire experience surreal. He knew he should stop. There was an insistent tap in his brain trying to remind him that what he was doing was improper. She was simply irresistible, as enchanting as the night itself.

He crushed her to him, his mouth melding with hers, and lost himself in the evening primrose scent of her, the feel of her silky hair against his fingers, and the soft press of her body against his. He ran his hands over the silk of her dress. By God, she melted against him, and arousal gripped him in its velvet clutches.

His mind sent him a luscious vision of leading her to his bedroom, pulling up her skirt, and having his way with her. Her breasts strained against the fabric of her dress. He longed to worship them with his hands and lips. If only he could pull the pins from that lovely black hair and wrap it around his hand.

Only the caress of a cool breeze across the back of his neck brought him to his senses. He steadied her on her feet and backed away, horrified. The kiss they'd just shared was anything but chaste. He'd be lucky if the woman didn't run from his presence right then.

Her fingers lifted to lightly brush her bottom lip, her chest rising and falling in a steady pant that matched his own.

"I owe you an apology—"

"Nothing about that kiss demands an apology," she blurted, and didn't that bring a smile to his face.

"Still, you are a woman in my care, unchaperoned after dark. As wild as la Nouvelle-Orléans is, if one of the priests saw us, I fear we'd both find ourselves in the confessional."

She giggled. "Your kind is so strange."

"My kind?"

She hesitated for a moment as if the question caught her off guard. "Where I come from, showing physical affection to a romantic interest is far more accepted."

Raised by pirates, he thought again.

Drawing a deep breath, she straightened herself, her gaze drifting over him. The impish grin she wore seemed to indicate the kiss was as mutual as he'd hoped. Should he kiss her again? He wanted to desperately. His cock was entirely set on the idea.

Considering it, he blinked twice, but he was distracted by the shadows gathered around her. They were casting themselves in the wrong direction based on the position of the moon. He darted another glance at the bright orb in the sky and then looked back at her.

He must have been mistaken. The shadows were perfectly normal now.

Putain, it must be his overwhelming desire for her messing with his mind. His cock twitched as he thought about kissing her again, but he held his ground. She may be willing, but he cared too much for her to ruin her. In fact, for the first time ever, he could envision a future married to this woman.

"Tell me more about the stars," she said, casting an intrigued smile his way. Was that her way of easing the tension that had grown between them? If so, it worked.

"I like to start at Polaris." He pointed out the bright twinkle above them, then moved on, mapping the constellations for her one by one. He talked about how the position of the stars changed over the course of the year and all he'd learned about the theories surrounding their existence and the phenomena he played witness to. The heavens held limitless fascination for him, and he found as he discussed his work, that she held a similar fascination. Isis was like no other woman he'd ever met. She was an eager and interested learner who asked the kinds of questions that made him analyze the things he thought he knew from a different angle.

"Do you sometimes look into the night sky and think there must be other worlds out there, other... realms waiting to be discovered?" She watched him intently, as if how he answered this question meant everything to her.

"There have to be," he said. "Why, la Nouvelle-Orléans was only discovered in 1682, but it was here long before that. Where we are in the vastness of space, our place among the stars, it's a small part of something incredibly expansive. There must be more."

Now, she was studying him, her deep blue eyes seemingly fathomless in the night. "And that doesn't scare you? You wouldn't mind being challenged by something new? Perhaps discovering new creatures or new worlds?"

He straightened. What a strange question. "No," he said, believing it to his soul. "I would find it exciting to discover something new. It speaks to who I am as a scientist."

"You are a true philosopher, Pierre," she said, glancing back at the moon. "What a welcome surprise to meet you here. I did not expect it."

His gaze settled on her lips again. "I feel the same way."

After a moment more, she said, "It's late, and I have a long ride back to our plantation."

"You don't live in the square?"

"*Non*. I thought I shared this when you helped me with the horses. We've secured a land grant for a parcel along the Mississippi to raise indigo."

"Indigo?" Fascinating. "I've grown it—mind, in the botanical garden as a scientific pursuit—but as of yet, no one has farmed it at any scale here. You may be the first to do so. The Jesuits have made a success of other crops, but their indigo production is negligible. I'm not surprised *Commissaire* Salmon charged you with its production. He's desperately wanted to expand the yield of the parish. It seems an unsurmountable undertaking for a small family such as yours, however. You must manage a significant number of slaves."

She raised her chin, seemingly disgusted by the idea. "I thank you for your concern, Pierre, but my family has always had a way with growing things, and we would not think of owning other human beings for our own comfort and profit."

He gaped, struck speechless. Although he agreed with her principles, in theory, there were practicalities to consider, and he'd never met anyone quite so opposed to the status quo.

"You are an intriguing woman, Isis."

She slanted him a wicked grin. "You have no idea."

He tried to think of a response to that and came up short. She challenged him on so many levels. How could he convince her to see him again?

Turning, she headed for the door and then the stairs. Pierre followed her into the night, calling for the stableboy to bring her horse. In the moonlit courtyard, they waited, the silence unspooling between them.

"Pierre?"

"Yes?"

"What was in the kegs? What is it you bring to the tavern?"

A grin spread across his face as he recognized his opportunity. "You must come back so I can show you."

Her face lit up, and didn't that just make his heart sing? "An engineer, an astronomer, a botanist, and something more?"

He arched an eyebrow. "As I said before, I am a man of many talents, Mademoiselle Tanglewood. You simply must see me again so that I may show them to you. Or perhaps next time, you will allow me to call on you at your plantation."

"No," she said quickly. "I will come to you." She lowered her chin. "I look forward to it."

With the flash of a crooked smile, she mounted her horse and headed for the gate. "It's been a pleasure, Pierre."

He opened the gates for her and said his goodbyes. "Henri," Pierre called for his stableboy.

"*Oui, monsieur?*"

"Take a horse and follow her to ensure she makes it home safely, but take care not to be seen."

"*Oui, monsieur.*"

Pierre waited as the boy quickly saddled his fastest steed and trotted out the gate. Meanwhile, he jogged back into the house, up the stairs, and to the telescope he'd just shown Isis, but instead of pointing it toward the sky, he swung the arm in search of her. He found Henri first, and then, a distance ahead of him, Isis. By the light of the moon, she traveled toward the river. He blinked when she passed into the shadow of a great oak tree—and never came out the other side. He swiveled the arm again, desperately searching for her. There was Henri, frantic. He'd lost her as well. Pierre lowered the viewer and then raised it to his eye again, scanning the entire area for any hint of her. Impossible. She was simply gone.

Returning to his courtyard, he waited for Henri. When the boy returned, his face was sickly white, and he dropped from the saddle with a lack of grace Pierre hadn't seen before in the boy. Breathlessly he reported, "The lady, monsieur! She disappeared."

Pierre didn't argue with the boy; he'd seen it himself. "I'm sure there's—"

"Like a specter! Even the horse's footprints ended in the shadows." The boy trembled with fear. "Do you think she is a witch?"

Everything in Pierre recoiled from the thought. "Of course not, Henri. Mademoiselle Tanglewood is a friend." He patted the boy on the back. "Moonlight can play tricks on the eyes." When the boy didn't seem to be soothed by his words, Pierre did something he rarely did; he lied. "I was watching, from the observatory. She turned right only a house-length past where you stopped. I think there is a rocky patch just there. You must have missed her."

Henri blinked twice. "You saw her continue on her way?"

"*Oui*. She didn't disappear, *garçon*. People don't just disappear."

Some color returned to the boy's cheeks, and his lips bent into a tentative smile. "Ah. I am sorry, *monsieur*, that I lost her trail."

He delivered two heavy thumps to the boy's back. "That's all right. Now, finish with the horses and off with you."

The boy gave a shallow bow and took off for the stables.

Pierre's smile faded once the boy was out of sight. He hated to lie, but a rumor of witchcraft could be deadly, and Isis Tanglewood did disappear. As God was his witness, she'd dissolved into thin air.

Early the next morning, Pierre woke to the sound of a woman screaming. He bound out of bed, dressed quickly, and headed in the direction of the sound, pulling on his boots on the way. Only when he made it to the center of town did he see the cause for alarm. A group had gathered in the square, and a large, gray lump lay between them. As he drew closer, he made out the body of a man and a familiar-looking waif of a woman with her hands raised to her mouth, who he supposed was the source of the scream.

He was relieved when the surgeon arrived on the scene. "Back away. Give us room," Viel ordered. He exchanged a dark look with Pierre as he lowered himself to the victim's side.

It was clear whatever had killed Guillaume had struck again. Two puncture wounds marred the neck of the corpse. Although no blood stained the pallid skin or the white sleeping shirt the man wore, Pierre thought the state of the corpse was too similar to the first to be a coincidence.

"Drained," Viel said under his breath, shaking his head.

Something about that sleep shirt bothered Pierre, but he couldn't wrap his mind around it.

Viel ordered a lieutenant nearby to inform the governor and to bring a cart for the remains. Someone else was dispatched to fetch a priest. Viel continued his examination, as questions piled up in Pierre's still-waking mind.

"Who is this man?" Pierre asked the slight woman whose screams had roused him.

Heaven help her, she looked ill. Her eyes were dull and listless, her dark hair limp, and her bare feet filthy from the dirt streets. "He's... my... husband," she said, the words broken with sobs.

Pierre couldn't miss the purplish bruise that blossomed beside her left eye or the round bruises that marred the wrist of the hand that gripped her handkerchief to her face. Whoever this was, her husband had been rough with her. He wondered how disappointed she could be that he'd met his fate.

"I'm sorry for your loss, Madame..."

"Cavalier. Lucienne Cavalier."

"How did this happen?" The man must have left his marriage bed at some point in the night. But Pierre had been watching this area when Isis left for home and searched it thoroughly once she'd disappeared. The murder must have occurred after that.

"Jacques said he'd heard something outside. He took the candle and went to check and never returned."

"You didn't go searching for him when he didn't come back to bed?"

"I fell asleep, *monsieur*. I only realized he was missing this morning and found him thus." She pointed a hand at her husband's corpse and blotted her eyes.

"Of course, I did not mean to upset you, *madame*, only

to understand the events of the night for some clue to what might have done this." Pierre walked around the body, noticing again how there was no blood on the nightshirt. No blood and no mud. His eyes went wide, and he focused on the man's bare feet. Now he realized what had bothered him before. Unlike his wife's, which were covered in dirt, Jacques's feet were clean, which meant the man had been... carried.

Pierre pictured a giant bird swooping down and lifting him off his plank wood porch. Icy realization skirted through him. He'd watched Isis disappear the night before not far from here. What if the same creature had taken her? She'd spoken of vampires. Wasn't the legend that they could fly? She'd been in this square only minutes before.

He had to find her and make sure she was okay.

He turned for the *ordinateur's* office.

"Where are you going?" Viel asked.

He cleared his throat. "To investigate along the river. If this is some kind of animal, there will be footprints."

Whether Viel was appeased by the explanation, Pierre couldn't be sure, but the priest arrived then, and the men turned their attention back to the body. Oh, Pierre did plan to check the riverbank for strange footprints, but first, he planned to find Isis and make sure she was okay. A quick visit to *Commissaire* Salmon and he had a map to the Tanglewood Plantation. The man kept records of each land grant, and as architect and engineer for the parish, Pierre had no trouble learning the precise location of the Tanglewoods'.

He rode at the fastest pace his horse could manage in the sweltering heat, following the water and then weaving through the thick forest. As it turned out, he didn't need to reference his map to know he was in the right place. A home the likes of which he hadn't seen since he left France rose at the top of a knoll, surrounded by oak trees. Behind it, a massive field of sprouting indigo stretched toward the swamp. He couldn't help but gape. True to her word, there wasn't a slave in sight, but the Tanglewoods had managed to build a plantation worthy of a king's visit in a matter of weeks.

His stomach dropped. This wasn't possible. It wasn't... natural. Could Henri have been right? Was Isis not a pirate as he'd assumed...but a *witch*? He tugged the reins and brought his horse to a stop, then took a long drink from his canteen. The heat must be getting to his head. Witches didn't exist. Neither did vampires.

"Are you here to see me?"

He almost fell off his horse. He hadn't heard her approach, but Isis stood in the shade of an oak tree to his right in a dress made of blue muslin that hugged her lovely figure like a whisper.

"I am," he said around his thickening tongue. Lord help him, she was beautiful. Despite his growing fear of her and the unknown that surrounded her, he found her utterly intriguing. The shadows seemed to cling to her within the shade of the mighty oak, and he was again reminded of how she resembled the night sky and fascinated him just the same.

"I thought I told you not to come here." She seemed almost annoyed at his intrusion. Then again, perhaps she didn't want him to see the plantation and the strange way it had erupted from nothing almost overnight.

"I came to make sure you made it home alive. I was concerned. There's been another murder."

Her expression darkened, and she lowered her chin to look at him through her lashes. "Another? Like before?"

"Completely drained of blood." His eyes locked with hers, and he was back on the terrace, kissing her. He wished he could pull her into his arms again now.

"I am well, as are my sisters and Rhys. But walk with me to the house and tell me about this tragedy." She took the horse's reins.

Some part of Pierre told him to turn his horse around and gallop away, but the unloyal beast seemed to be as enthralled with her as he was. The horse touched his muzzle to Isis's cheek, and she gave him an affectionate pat on his neck. Lucky steed. He dismounted and followed her. He was a man of science after all. Whatever had happened, her sudden disappearance and even more sudden appearance here beside him, there had to be a logical explanation.

"Your home is grand," he said as she tied the horse to a post in the shade of mature oak tree. She led Pierre up three steps to a large wood-and-brick building with a wrap-around porch and a roof made from stone shingles. He'd never seen such craftsmanship, and the design was both foreign to him and fascinating to his architect's mind. "How?" he mumbled.

"Come in, Pierre. Have something to drink."

She led him to a dining room with a large, glassless window, whose shutters had been thrown open, bathing the room in fresh air. "Please." She gestured toward a chair. "I'll return with tea."

It was remarkably comfortable in the room, at least ten degrees cooler than outdoors, and his shoulders released some of the tension he'd been carrying since that morning. Most certainly, there was a logical explanation for Isis's disappearance last night, and she couldn't have had anything to do with the murder. Not her. Someone so lovely was incapable of such a crime.

Casually, he strode to the window, coupling his hands behind his back. His gaze caught on a fly then, beyond the boundaries of the room. He concentrated on it as it flew toward him, then reversed direction. Odd. Oh! It wasn't flying backward; it was bouncing! Confused, he reached through the opening in the wall and brushed it away. Other insects—mosquitos and gnats—landed on his hand and forearm. As he pulled his hand back, every one of them stripped off and stayed on the other side of what he was beginning to realize was an invisible barrier of some kind. He whirled, inspecting the room. Not a single bug or bird buzzed inside, although a soft breeze fluttered the tablecloth.

Pierre examined the evidence before him as he might a scientific experiment. The tablecloth was made of fine linen and set with a silver candelabra and a bowl of fresh oranges. They'd left town on horseback, without so much as a cart, only weeks ago. He'd arrived here on horseback. There wasn't a road wide enough for a cart. So, how did they fully furnish this house so quickly? How did they build it? None of this made sense. It wasn't possible. He pinched the flesh between his thumb and forefinger, trying to wake himself up. Definitely awake. Which meant... Which meant...

Isis returned with a silver tray loaded with bone china cups, macarons, cheeses, baguettes, and jam. She set it on the table, her dress shifting against her curves like something out of an erotic dream.

"I hope this blend suits. It's Circe's favorite and the only thing I had on hand." She turned over the cups and poured. "Sugar?"

Pierre's mouth was dry as a stone. "How did you prepare this so quickly without a servant?"

"My sister already had water on the stove."

"And how is it that you have a stove? How did you come by it?"

She frowned. "Have you been watching us day and night? How would you know what we have brought and what we have not?"

She sounded defensive, but he had to get this out. He had to know the truth. "No one could build this house in the short time you've been here. The roof itself would require hundreds of man-hours, and you have no slaves and no servants." He turned and pointed toward the space in the wall. "The insects cannot enter this room. This table, these candlesticks...they are in pristine condition. Like new! Not things transported from a great distance over rough terrain." He searched her face. "And you... You, Isis, you come and go, appearing and disappearing from thin air."

She brushed a hand down the front of her dress. "You seem to have examined me thoroughly, Pierre. What conclusions have you drawn?"

"You are an enchantress who has enslaved my heart."

Lowering herself into the chair across the table, she crossed her legs and leaned toward him, her deep blue eyes made brighter by the light shining in, turning her pupils to dark pinpoints. All at once, she burst into laughter, the wild sound filling the room. "Enslaved your heart?" She raised an eyebrow. "That, I have not done, Pierre. If you are a slave to me, I am sorry to inform you that you've given yourself to me of your own volition. I'm happy to accept your service. I find you enchanting and enslaving as well." She shifted in her seat. "In fact, I find myself doing the most foolish things to be near you, like inviting you here, for example, when I should have turned you away at the border of my property."

He stared at her, waiting for further explanation, but she said nothing. She almost looked...conflicted.

"Sit, Pierre. The tea is not going to drink itself, and you need it after your ride here. You were going to tell me what happened in town this morning." She patted the table across from her.

Almost as if he were in a dream, he lowered himself into the chair. "Then, it wasn't you who did it?"

She leaned back in her chair. "Did what?"

"Murder the man who was found this morning?"

Her body jolted as if he'd hit her. "No, I haven't murdered anyone," she said through a frown. "I was with you, and then I was here." Her voice was harder now, as if she took offense at the accusation.

"But you can see why I'd think it was you." He held a hand toward her.

"*Non*, I'm afraid I don't see."

"What is a man supposed to think? I was watching you last night from my observatory, Isis. I saw you... disappear. You stepped into a shadow and never stepped out."

"You were watching me? How incredibly rude!"

He ignored the protest. "The man this morning was drained of all his blood, just like the last one, and his body was left near to where you disappeared. Nothing like this has ever happened in *la Nouvelle-Orléans* until now... Until you arrived!"

"Another one." She sipped her tea and blew out a heavy breath. "I thought the vampire might strike again, but I didn't think it would be so soon."

"Vampires! Again, this talk of them." He flipped a hand through the air dismissively.

"A vampiric creature is the most likely perpetrator." She shrugged.

"I am a man of science, Isis! I am telling you, they do not exist!" His outburst hung in the air around them. Her expression seemed nonplussed, until, after what might have been a full minute, she gathered herself and asked, "Sugar?"

He glanced down at his steaming cup of tea. "No, thank you."

Pointing a finger at the sugar cubes on the table, she rotated her wrist. The cube rose in the air, floated to her cup, and plunged into her tea. Another circle of her finger and the spoon began to stir within the cup, without her touching it.

Pierre blinked at her, then at the cup.

"Tell me, man of science, do I exist?"

CHAPTER
TEN

She'd gone and done it now. Isis watched Pierre's face turn bloodless and wondered if she'd made a terrible mistake. Everything in her told her she could trust the man, but if she was wrong, she'd have to take drastic steps. She'd promised her sisters she'd hide her powers. Medea would throw a fit if she knew what Isis had done. If Pierre proved unworthy of her secret, she'd have no choice but to wipe his fragile mind. Oh, how she'd loathe to do so. The man was clearly brilliant; his brain contained a delicate network of interconnected knowledge. Along with removing his visit to Tanglewood Plantation, she'd risk removing other memories. Other...connections.

"You are real," he said softly, swallowing hard. "But I think... not human."

That made her laugh. "I am human—" she began, and his body sagged from relief. "But not the same kind of human you are."

The tension was back, and she saw his hand tremble where it rested on the table, the cup beside it rattling in its saucer.

GENEVIEVE JACK

"Don't be afraid." She held up her hands, searching her mind for a way to explain to him so that he would understand. "You're a man of science, and you've studied the stars. You told me you have wondered... You have considered that there is something else out there, something beyond what you understand to be true."

He swallowed nervously. "Are you from the stars?"

She tipped her head, considering. "I am from a parallel dimension. There are universes, Pierre, realities happening at the same time as your own, like two ships sailing across an open sea but at a distance, never to meet, never to know that the other existed."

For a long time, he just stared at her, eyes abnormally wide, until he reached for his teacup, as if he needed a drink to steady his nerves. He took a sip, the liquid sloshing slightly in his trembling grip, then closed his eyes as if savoring the flavor. "This tea is delicious. I've never had a finer cup."

"Thank you." She winked at him, and he examined the cup again, clearly uneasy with the idea that magic might have been involved in its making. Well, she wouldn't apologize for that.

"Do all humans from your... realm do magic?" he asked, and Isis could almost see the emotions warring within him. He was afraid; undeniably, the fear was there, but he was also curious, and the curiosity sparking in those sharp, intelligent eyes was far stronger than the fear. She'd known it would be when he'd kissed her last night and then spoke of the stars as if he longed to explore the heavens. He was a man who lived to discover, and she was giving him a great unknown.

"*Oui*," she said simply. "All humans on Ouros are witches or wizards."

He jerked back. "Then you are a witch."

She couldn't contain her laugh. "Yes, but that word is different where I come from. It might be how you would describe yourself as French. It is what we are, not what we do. My power comes from my heritage, not from any devil or demon." *Not usually anyway.* She had encountered demons using magic, but Pierre needn't know about that.

Visibly perplexed, he studied her. "Tell me about Ouros."

"There are other creatures there, elves, fairies, dragons, and vampires."

"Vampires..."

"*Oui.* That is how I know what murdered those two men. Vampires exist where I come from, and they drain their victims of their blood, just like those men were drained."

Seemingly agitated, Pierre stood from his chair and paced to the window where a fly battered against the magic that protected the room. Isis hated the way Pierre stared at that fly. That was the thing about the lower life forms on this world; the fly's mind could not process magic, and so its impulses were caught on repeat, its wings beating fruitlessly against the force that kept it out until it grew exhausted and dropped to its death. Goddess, what was this experience doing to Pierre?

"I am trusting you with this, Pierre, because I can see you are an intellectual, a philosopher, a man of discovery. I am trusting you with my secret so we can move beyond it." Couldn't he see she'd practically placed her heart on a platter and handed it to him with his tea?

He whirled to face her. "Tell me this, Isis. Did the vampire follow you from your...realm?"

Her shoulders relaxed a little. That was a good question

—a question by a logical, believing mind. "No. The way we came was guarded. We are the only ones to come through. I think this vampire is indigenous to this land. I was hoping you'd have heard legends among the people who were here before."

"The Indians? I can't claim to understand their language well, but I have known a few who have managed to learn French. I've never heard any story like that."

"Hmm." Isis sipped her tea, the hot, sweet liquid coursing down her throat. Delphine's image popped into her head, young and beautiful again, when only days before she'd been so ill. Vampires where Isis came from were born and not made, but perhaps things worked differently here. "Tell me, Pierre, have you seen much of Mrs. Devereaux—I mean Laurent—since her husband was murdered?"

"I can't say that I have. The last time I saw her was the day he was found dead."

Delphine was still Isis's primary suspect, but she needed more proof before she started accusing her, even to Pierre. "I'll talk to her. Maybe she knows more about her husband's death than she's willing to tell men of authority."

"Brilliant idea." He finished what was in his cup.

"Was the man who was killed today married?"

"*Oui.* His wife, Lucienne, found his body."

"Lucienne?" Where had she heard that name before?

He nodded.

A memory jarred loose, and she inhaled deeply. "Delphine's sister."

"Hmm?"

"Lucienne is Delphine's sister. Their maiden name is Devereaux."

Pierre seemed startled by this. "Now that you mention it, I noticed the resemblance. Do these vampires you know of tend to torment specific families?"

A vision of Delphine, flawless and otherworldly, in the tavern the night before came to mind, and Isis bristled. "Not usually, but I think creatures are different here."

"These are strange times, indeed," he mumbled.

"Pierre, can I count on you to keep my secret?" she asked again. "Others might not understand."

He sat up straighter. "They wouldn't understand. You must know that. There are those who believe even my telescope is an affront to God's plan. But you have nothing to fear from me. What you've told me today, and what I've seen here, I will keep in confidence."

"Thank you."

"On one condition."

She looked at him expectantly.

"You must return to my home for another visit and allow me to show you what was in those barrels." He gave her a wolfish grin.

She quirked an eyebrow. "Are you suggesting your silence can only be bought with my company?"

A twinkle in his eye accompanied his answer. "For starters. I count myself among the lucky to have such leverage. Only a fool wouldn't use it."

"Only a fool would believe using it would gain my favor." She laughed.

The room grew quiet. Pierre tapped his fingers on the table as if he were deliberating something. She was about to ask him if he was all right when he sprang from his chair, rounded the table, and abruptly yanked her up and into his arms. It was all too easy to mold her body to his when he looked at her like that, like he was in total control and knew exactly what he wanted, and that thing was *her*.

"What *would* gain your favor, Isis?" His breath skated across her cheek, and his eyes fixated on her lips. "I am a man of many talents. Would you like the moon? I can't pull it down for you, but I can show it to you in a way no other man can."

Magic rose within her. Or she thought it must be magic. A rush like lightning branched and sizzled in her core, pounding in her veins. Her heart beat a mad tattoo against her breastbone.

"Aren't you afraid of me?" she asked breathlessly. "I just admitted to you that I'm not of this world. I showed you magic for the first time and told you there's a blood-sucking monster in your midst."

He held her tighter, his hard length evident against her hip. "No, I'm not afraid. I must be crazy not to be, and it's a crazy thing to do, taking you into my arms. Have you cast a spell over me, Isis? Because I find that despite knowing that I should be afraid, and feeling apprehensive only moments ago, what I feel now has nothing to do with fear."

Heavy-lidded, she watched him through her lashes. Her breasts plumped, and a delicious ache throbbed between her legs. Shadows swirled around her ankles with her excitement. "We are alone. Why don't you show me?"

At her invitation, he slid his hands up her sides and buried his fingers in her hair. "I thought you'd never ask."

OF ALL THE RECKLESS THINGS PIERRE HAD DONE IN HIS LIFE, THIS might be the pinnacle. The woman was a witch. She'd said it plainly enough. Even now, as he kissed her full red lips, an unnatural coolness entered the room as if the night itself had seeped in and was ruffling his shirt. The chill felt good against his skin. Isis made him burn. He thought he might combust if he didn't have her.

"Is this part of our deal, to keep my secret?" she asked suddenly.

"No," he said, pulling his hands from her and backing away. "Isis, I would never... You always have a choice."

"I thought your religion here forbade the pleasures of the flesh outside of marriage."

He cocked his head. "I've never been a particularly religious man. Is that how it is where you are from?"

She shook her head. "No. I have had a lover."

Lover. And why did he suddenly want to kill whoever it was? "Do you want me to stop?"

Her breath came out in a heavy sigh. "No. I want you to show me how you feel. I want you to teach me how a man from this realm touches a woman he wants. That is, if you want me."

"Oh, there is no denying that, sweet Isis." He traced his fingers along the neck of her gown, cupping her breast through the thin material. Yanking the fabric down, he freed her luscious mounds, the dress supporting them underneath. Damn him, they were as perfect as they appeared through the fabric. He lowered his head and sucked one of her perfect rose-colored nipples into his mouth. She arched against him and moaned.

Faintly, he was aware of the room growing darker, as if a storm was moving in. Good. Let it rain. He planned to be inside for a good while.

He moved his hand to take over where his mouth left off, rolling her nipple between his thumb and forefinger, and triumphed at the delicious sounds of pleasure it elicited. Drawing her left breast into his mouth, he did the same to it, rolling the tight bud over his tongue, sucking gently. She leaned more fully into his arms.

Oh, to watch her come apart. From the moment he'd met her, he'd wondered how so much power and confidence could be housed in one woman's body. Now, he knew she was no ordinary woman, and he longed to take her apart and put her back together, to see all her working parts.

He bunched the fabric of her skirt toward her hip, working it higher until he reached the hem. A shift of his leg between hers and he'd pinned the fabric in place, freeing his palm to press flush against her inner thigh. The silken feel of her skin was almost his undoing. His cock throbbed as he stroked up her leg, slowly following the soft curve of her thigh until he reached her bare center.

"You're so wet." His fingers glided along her slit, and he broke from the kiss to watch her reaction. Her lips were swollen, her pupils wide, turning her eyes dark. Her nails scraped along the fabric covering his chest.

She moved to remove his shirt.

"Not yet, goddess. Let me watch you." He slipped a finger into her wet folds, then another when she arched against his hold. He made a come-to-me gesture with his fingers inside her, circling against her inner wall while the heel of his palm cupped her between her legs. Hunger and desire played across her face, and he smiled as he took her breast into his mouth again, suckling as he increased the speed of his fingers. She rode his hand in the most erotic way, grinding against his touch, chasing her release.

Something caressed the inside of his ankle. It felt like cool fingers, but both her hands were still fisting his shirt. Startled, he gave his leg a shake, breaking the rhythm.

"Don't stop," she gasped. "It's me. My magic."

Heart pounding, he pushed all fear aside, focusing only on her as he started again, working his hand deeper into her, laving her breasts with his tongue.

The caress continued, featherlight up the inside of his thigh. He groaned against her when the cool caress reached his balls and fondled them with exquisite pressure. This was new. He marveled at the feeling as it wrapped around his cock. It was like the night itself had taken him into its mouth. He thrust against her, his hand working between them, inside her.

He increased his pace as the magic increased in intensity. Sucking, licking, stroking, swirling along the head of his cock. He glanced between them, shocked his clothes were still on. He felt naked, exposed to the night that had seeped in around them. The room was thick with it now, the only light from the candles flickering on the table.

He circled his thumb over her clit, increasing the speed and pressure even as his own body threatened to pitch him over that glorious peak. When she tossed her head back and cried out, her inner walls pulsing against his fingers, he was not far behind. The magic tightened around his cock one last time, and he emptied himself into it, bending his knees to absorb the aftershocks that rocked through them both.

Later, through the haze of ecstasy, awareness dawned. Shadows circled the room. Slowly, the inky darkness seemed to leak back into Isis, as if she were drawing her own shadow into herself. The light returned, and the sounds of birds and buzzing things filled the space that was previously silent. He gaped as the last tendril of darkness flowed like blood from the toe of his boot back into her.

"I do like your ways here," she whispered against his lips.

Why wasn't he afraid? This was by far the most bizarre and potentially terrifying experience of his life, yet all his brain could produce was a desire to have her again.

"Isis!"

Pierre slipped his hand from under her skirt and stepped back at the sight of Isis's sister standing in the doorway. The woman was clearly angry, her eyes sparking with mystical light.

Isis righted her dress, covering her breasts and smoothing her skirt over her legs. "I thought you were in the fields."

"We finished early," she snapped.

"You must be Medea," Pierre said, trying to force his voice to remain friendly. He thought about offering her his hand but then realized he'd just withdrawn it from under her sister's skirt and, instead, coupled it behind his back and gave a shallow bow. "I am Pierre Baron. Pleasure to meet you."

Medea gave him a curt nod before turning a biting glare on Isis. "May I speak with you in the other room, sister?"

Isis smoothed her hair and then her dress. "Pierre and I were just saying goodbye. I'll meet you there in a moment."

Medea turned on her heel and left.

"I will go," Pierre said. "I can see I've caused you some trouble."

Isis shook her head. "Don't worry about her. May I come and visit you, tomorrow night?"

"It's safer during the day," he said.

She gave him a wicked grin. "Not for me."

He placed a kiss upon her cheek. "Then come. I'll be waiting."

He slipped out the door, finding his horse rested and watered, waiting in the shade of the oak tree. He tried to capture it all with his mind so he could sketch it in his journal later. How he longed to learn more, to remember everything. How he ached for more fascinating, mysterious Isis.

CHAPTER
ELEVEN

"**H**ave you lost your mind?" Medea paced the salon, clenching and unclenching her fists.

Isis bristled. She didn't care for her sister's tone. "Pierre came to tell me of another vampire victim. He sought us out to make sure I was okay."

"What I saw when I walked into that room... Was that your way of thanking him?" Medea scoffed at her.

Isis stood straighter, hands on her hips, and raised her chin. "No. We were through talking about vampires by that point, but I find him quite handsome and don't regret a single thing. That man may study me any way and anywhere he pleases." She giggled.

Medea winced. "Goddess, Isis! We just left a happy home in France because the people there wanted to burn us alive! Are you so anxious to repeat the experience?" She waved a hand overhead. "Do you love the smell of torches in the morning?"

The laugh that pealed from Isis's chest filled the room. "Relax, sister. I swear to you, Pierre will not betray me. The man is enamored. He wouldn't do anything to hurt me."

"For now." Medea's face fell, and she released a deep sigh. "You do realize that if this goes wrong, you put us all in danger. Not just yourself. All of us."

Sobering, Isis approached her sister and placed a hand over her heart. "I promise you, if he turns out to be a problem, I'll wipe his mind myself. Honestly, I believe the greater threat is the vampire he came to warn me about."

"You say the creature struck again?"

"Yes, Medea, and I confirmed that these are the first killings of this type on record here. Pierre studies the animals and fauna in this area. Even among the indigenous people, he's heard no stories supporting the existence of local vampires until now."

Medea's hands pressed into her stomach. "I don't like this. Why was the first man left in a tree on our property? You don't think..." She pressed her lips together.

"That a vampire followed us here from Ouros? No. However, I think, possibly, one came on the same boat as us."

Medea's eyes narrowed. "What do you know?"

"Do you remember the woman who begged me to intervene when we disembarked?"

"I do."

"Her name is Delphine, and her husband was the first to die. I saw her last night at the tavern, and she was positively transformed from her previous sickly state to a supernatural beauty. And the man Pierre told me about this morning was Lucienne's husband. Lucienne is Delphine's sister."

Medea thought about it for a moment. "*Fuck*. How? She was human when she stepped off that ship. I saw her in the light of day."

"I don't know, but I intend to pay Delphine a visit and find out."

A fresh breath of air filled the room, like a morning breeze through dewy spring leaves, and Circe appeared, smiling in the doorway. Well, her belly appeared first. She was ever rounder each day now, the baby due in less than two weeks' time. "What's going on in here?"

Isis exchanged glances with Medea and hooked her pinkie inside her sister's. *No need to stress her about the killings.* Reading one another's thoughts was a talent the three sisters had been honing over the years. It was much easier to send the thought to Medea than to keep it from Circe.

"Isis has taken a lover," Medea blurted. "I was just warning her about the consequences."

Circe squealed and held her arms open to Isis for a hug. "Oh, honey! Tell me all about him."

Medea left the room, rolling her eyes.

THE NEXT AFTERNOON, ISIS HEADED INTO TOWN TO VISIT WITH Delphine Devereaux. Traveling at night would have been easier for her, but this visit during the heart of the day held purpose. Vampires in Ouros experienced the sleep of the dead when the sun was up. According to Pierre, he'd seen Delphine the morning after her husband died, and she'd been human when Isis had met her on the ship. Either vampirism worked differently in this realm, or they were mistaken about Delphine and there was another explanation for her change in appearance. Either way, Isis planned to find out what her role was in all of this.

Thankfully, the death of Guillaume Laurent gave her the perfect excuse to visit Delphine. With a basket of goodies on her hip, Isis proceeded to the former Laurent residence under the guise of bringing a meal to a grieving widow and gave the home's wooden door a firm knock. No answer. She knocked again. A thud sounded inside, as if something heavy had fallen off a shelf. Finally, footsteps. The door opened only a crack.

"Can I help you?" A young woman's face appeared in the gap, her straight hair the color of ripe wheat. She looked familiar. Delphine's youngest sister? What was her name? Isis couldn't remember.

"Is Delphine here? The priest told me this was her home. I heard her husband passed and came to bring her a few things." She held up the basket, brimming with freshly baked bread and smoked meats.

"That's kind of you. I'm her sister Antoinette. I can give it to her." She held out her hand.

Isis turned her body to move the basket out of reach. "May I see her? I'd like to convey my condolences myself."

Antoinette turned her head, glancing inside the house. "She's not taking visitors. You probably haven't heard yet that our sister Lucienne lost her husband only yesterday to the same fever that killed Delphine's husband. I'm afraid she's crippled with grief. Delphine is tending to her and is, I'm afraid, in no condition to entertain guests."

Fever. That was an interesting spin. A whisper reached Isis's ear, the sound of a shadow trying to get her attention. Her magic reached out for it, and she searched the dark interior behind Antoinette. "In that case, please give this to her and tell her that Isis Tanglewood sends her deepest sympathy." She shoved the wide basket at Antoinette, sticking her toe inside when the young girl opened the door wider to her. The shadow bit into her boot and melted icily through her skin. She stepped back again.

The door closed in her face, but it was too late. Images flashed in her mind, her magic wringing them from the shadows. Lucienne lay on a simple bed, deathly pale and thin. Delphine knelt beside her, bending over her as if in prayer. Perhaps what Antoinette said was true. Could Isis have been mistaken about Delphine being responsible for the deaths?

Another image flashed in her mind, Delphine raising her head. Isis gasped. Her skin was marble white, and her eyes glowed pale in the dim light. On the ship, Delphine's eyes had been brown. She remembered as much. Now, they were too similar to Master Demidicus's, the vampire who had helped them escape Paragon.

Everything in her believed Delphine was a vampire and the murderer, but she had to think what to do about it. She strolled the streets, pondering her next move. She had to get Delphine alone, confront her, make her understand she could not kill here again. Isis stopped short when a shop window caught her eye. Not the window itself but what was behind it, a perfect emerald of a cut she hadn't seen since her time in Darnuith. She hadn't known the people of this realm capable of such craftsmanship.

She tipped her head back and looked up at the sign: BLAKEMORE'S IMPORTS. Curious, she walked through the open door into the shady interior. The shop had all manner of goods—furniture, jewelry, bolts of fabric. She ran her hand along a particularly fine length of silk. This was not made here. Whoever owned this shop must have had it shipped in from the old world.

"Can I help you?"

Isis whirled at the voice and froze. Of all the things she'd expected to come face-to-face with in this wild, untamed corner of the globe, this was the last of them. A dragon, here, in la Nouvelle-Orléans.

CHAPTER
TWELVE

"I'm sorry... Have we met before?" The smoky scent of the dragon met her nose, and she examined him, disbelieving what was right in front of her. His illusion was good; she'd give him that. He appeared before her, a tall, dark human in contemporary finery. But all the signs were there. His unusually large size, the way his eyes reflected light more like a cat's than a human's, and this place, he was standing amid his own stash of treasure.

"No," she said quickly. "I was just admiring your inventory." Standing in the man's proximity was like being in the shadow of a mountain. The aura of a warrior surrounded him. Isis knew her own power and, even so, was intimidated by his presence. She watched his nostrils flare and the smile fade from his lips.

Rounding the crowded room, he kept his distance while making his way toward the front of the store. "Is there anything I can help you find?" he asked, but his voice was wooden. She sized him up, and he did the same to her. Who was more afraid of whom?

"I was wondering where you obtained the emerald in

the window and the one on your finger," she asked, pointedly gazing at his large emerald ring. That piece of jewelry was charged with so much magic she could almost taste it. She knew what it meant, what he was.

He kept moving until he reached the door, and she realized too late he was closing it, locking it, placing his body between her and freedom. "What brings you here, *witch*?"

She should have known it would be impossible to hide what she was from him. "I should ask you the same, *dragon*."

"Who are you?" he asked.

When she had left Ouros with her sisters, Paragon had initiated a smear campaign against witches. Time was a funny thing. Time in Ouros and time on Earth ran at two different speeds, sometimes rushing forward like a raging river and other times as meandering as a shallow stream. Without knowing when the dragon left Paragon for this realm, she couldn't be sure if she was safe sharing the truth about their circumstances. Medea had been queen of Darnuith. Eleanor and Brynhoff thought she was dead. Although Isis and Circe did not suffer the defamation that their sister did, people knew who they were at the time of their leaving, and most dragons either feared or hated them. She was in no hurry to find out if this dragon was one of them.

"Someone who means you no harm," she said finally, raising her chin. "My family and I came here to live a peaceful existence away from the strife and turmoil we experienced in Darnuith."

"Then you are from Paragon," he said, and she tried not to wince. The realm they were from was once called Ouros. Paragon, the kingdom of dragons, was just one of the five kingdoms that made up the continent. The kingdom of the witches, Darnuith, where she was from, was another. But Eleanor had always spoken of uniting the kingdoms under Paragonian rule. This dragon's words suggested she'd succeeded.

Isis lowered her chin. "Yes. I assume you came here for the same reason... to escape the politics of the region. A dragon such as yourself wouldn't have left Paragon without cause."

"No." Invisible walls went up between them. She'd touched a raw nerve. Interesting. He brushed the perfectly tailored sleeve of his jacket with his hand, although there wasn't a speck of dust or wrinkle to smooth. His eyes narrowed. Knees slightly bent, Gabriel's hulking body seemed coiled tight, ready to spring. "My reasons for leaving are my own. As for how I ended up here, specifically... Well, that is a long story for another time. I must confess, this is the last place I thought I'd ever find a witch from Darnuith."

"Likewise. Although I'm beginning to believe there are more supernatural creatures in this small parish than I bargained for."

His eyebrows lifted. "There is magic here," he said in a low voice, gritty as if coated with cinders. "Magic that is not of our realm. Different... unexpected magic."

Isis frowned. "You suspect a vampire as well?"

"Among other things." His gaze drifted toward the front window.

"I know our kind has not always aligned easily with each other, but perhaps, under these circumstances, we could be friends."

He stroked his chin, his eyes burning darkly. "I think only time will tell if we will be friends, but I am willing to be allies. Although I must warn you, the people here may be surrounded by the supernatural, but they are not receptive to it. One whiff of it and they will kill what they do not understand. What we are must remain hidden at all costs."

She nodded, thinking of Pierre, the trust she'd placed in him taking on new weight at Gabriel's words. "Agreed. Your confidence is secure with me and my family."

"Your family?"

"There are four of us here."

He ran a hand down his face. "Goddess help us."

"May I go?" she pointed at the door.

He held out one massive hand. "Gabriel."

She shook it. "Isis."

He bowed at the waist, then opened the door and ushered her into the muggy afternoon heat.

SHE WAS STILL THINKING ABOUT THE DRAGON AND HIS PLACE IN dragon society when she was guided through the gate of Pierre's home by a dark-skinned woman named Allyette who rushed off to find Pierre. Why had Gabriel come to this world? Why here? She pushed aside those thoughts when Pierre swept through the front door, a puckish grin she was becoming enamored with spreading his lips. "Isis Tanglewood, in the light of day. What a pleasure."

Goddess, the way he moved filled her with fire. She remembered the feeling of being wrapped in those well-corded arms and drew a deep breath to center herself. "I had business in town. I hope you don't mind my arriving early." She winked.

"Not at all," he said in a low, sultry whisper, darkening eyes staring at her through his lashes. "You can come anytime. Why, come now, come later, stay the night if you wish and be here first thing in the morning, ready to come again."

A blush climbed her cheeks. "You have a filthy mouth, Monsieur Baron. Shall we go inside so I might show you what to do with it?"

His eyes turned stormy, and he placed a hand in the center of her back. "As much as I'd enjoy that particular lesson, there is something I have to do first, and it fulfills a promise I made to you earlier."

"Lead the way. I have something to share with you as well."

He moved toward a large shed on the edge of his court-yard while she told him about her visit to Delphine's. She left out the part about Blakemore's. She'd promised the dragon to keep his true identity a secret, and she would.

"You think Delphine is responsible for her husband's death?" Pierre's brows knit. "She's the..."

"Vampire," Isis said, noticing the way he cringed slightly at the word.

"Please excuse me. I fear the scientist in me is still resistant to the idea of magical beings."

She flashed him a wicked smile. "Do I need to prove it to you again?"

His eyes turned hooded, and he opened the door for her. "First, let me show you a little magic of my own."

Inside, kegs were stacked against one wall across from a wood-burning stove with a giant, capped cauldron atop it. A pipe ran from the top of the sealed cauldron to a copper vat. "What is this, Pierre?"

"Science of a different kind." He pulled a small glass from his pocket and opened the tap on one of the barrels. Clear amber liquid poured into the glass, and he handed it to her.

She sniffed it, alcohol vapors singeing her nose. With a lift of her eyebrow, she tried a sip, coughing as the burn traveled from her throat to her toes. She giggled. "I've never tried this sort of brandy. It's...strong."

"That's because it's not brandy. It's rum, made from molasses, not fruit."

"Molasses? Plantations in Haiti feed it to their pigs."

His eyes twinkled as he took another sip. "They send it to me for the cost of getting it here. I ferment it and sell it to Touze. It's proven popular."

She tossed back the rest. This time, the burn didn't catch her off guard as before, and a delicious buzz made her smile. "I can see why. It's stronger than tribiscal wine."

"What's tribiscal wine?"

She handed him back the empty glass, and he refilled it. "Where I come from, it's a dark purple fruit, similar to your grape but larger. It grows on trees. And when it is fermented, it's extremely intoxicating to witches."

His expression grew serious. "This place you're from sounds beautiful."

Memories of Darnuith came back to her, and her eyes brimmed with tears. She took another sip of rum. "It is. Our kingdom rises from whitecapped mountains where it's always winter. We travel in sleighs pulled by massive hounds, bigger than any dogs you have in this realm."

"Sounds brutal."

She laughs. "No. We all have magic, so the places we want or need to be warm are. Every season you have here, we also have there, exactly where and when we need them. But beyond the magic, there is ice and snow. It protects us."

He studied her, his silvery-gray eyes flicking between her features. "It sounds like a botanist's dream."

She grinned. "I'm sure you'd enjoy yourself. I should introduce you to Rhys. He was an apothecary in Darnuith."

"Darnuith. That's the name of where you are from?"

She nodded. "Medea would kill me if she knew I was telling you this." She glanced down at the drink in her hands. "Is there truth serum in rum?"

He chuckled. "In all alcohol, I fear." A refreshing breeze blew through the door, and Isis turned her face to it, smiling at the way the cool air tickled her skin. Dark clouds had moved in, and she smelled rain, although it hadn't begun to fall.

"I shouldn't be telling you so much," she said.

"You can trust me, Isis. I want to know everything about you. Everything that crosses your mind." He moved in closer and tucked a strand of hair behind her ear. "Why did you leave Darnuith?"

"We were fleeing political unrest." That seemed like a safe enough explanation. He wouldn't understand the details anyway.

He sipped his drink again, a frown following his swallow. "I'm sad to hear there is no dimension free of the threat of war."

She chewed her lip. "You're right about that. Hate is universal, unfortunately. It transcends time and space and exists in every dimension."

He gripped her chin, his body close, his eyes hooded. "What about love? Does that exist in every dimension too?"

The corners of her mouth lifted of their own accord. "I've heard it does. I've observed as much."

"But you've never experienced it for yourself?"

Goddess, the heat coming off his body, coupled with the cool breeze and the bite of the rum, had created an intoxicating swell within her. "No," she said softly.

He lowered his mouth closer to hers. "Don't you think we should rectify that? I mean, for scientific purposes."

A crack of thunder rumbled through them. The rain came then, falling in fast and vigorous sheets that hit the ground with a vengeance. The wind blew a gust of rain into the distillery, spraying them, and she shrieked with laughter. Pierre released her chin to run to close the door, drowning them in darkness.

"Stay there. I'll find a candle," Pierre said.

"*Fotiá*," Isis whispered, and the tip of her wand glowed to life and bathed the room in a warm light.

Lips parted in wonder, Pierre marveled at her spell. "That's a neat trick."

"Take my hand, and I'll show you another." She extended her fingers toward him, and he didn't hesitate. As soon as his hand was in hers, she called the shadows to carry them away.

Still clinging to her, Pierre gasped when they materialized in the main room of his home. His eyes had widened to the size of saucers but still held the edge of fascination.

"Are you okay?" she asked with concern. "You're very pale."

"Yes." He swallowed, licking his lips as if his mouth had gone dry. "I just... I didn't know you could do that. You're very powerful."

The clatter of a metal tray hitting the floor sent them whirling.

"Allyette..." Pierre reached toward the dark-skinned servant.

The woman crossed herself and said something in her native tongue that Isis didn't understand.

"Are you all right?" Pierre rushed toward her, hands up,

but Allyette was backing away, fear in her eyes as if she'd seen the devil himself.

This wouldn't do. Isis chastised herself for her poor decision to travel by shadow into the room. She should have remembered there were servants here, but she was tipsy from the rum and it had become difficult to think clearly. Still, it had happened. They'd been seen. Allyette could not be allowed to leave this room. If she relayed what happened to the wrong person...

Isis muttered a spell and cast a purple flare of light toward the woman. Allyette's face went slack. "You saw nothing. You remember nothing," she said, raising her wand.

"I saw nothing," Allyette repeated.

Isis lowered her wand and slipped it back into the sleeve of her dress. The woman's eyes darted around the room as if she didn't know where she was. "Are you well, Allyette?" Isis asked sweetly.

"I can't remember why I came in here," she mumbled.

Isis gave a soft laugh. "You offered to bring us tea just now. Don't you remember?" She picked up the tray and placed it back in her hands.

Allyette curtsied. "*Oui, Mademoiselle*. Right away." She disappeared in the direction of the kitchen.

Pierre gaped at her, then backed away, hands shaking.

She reached for him, but he dodged her touch. "You did something to her mind."

"I made her forget," she admitted.

"Have you ever done that to me?"

"No." She moved closer, but Pierre backed away in equal measure, keeping space between them. "Pierre?"

"You put Allyette into a stupor. If the magic you used in the distillery showed how powerful you are, this magic shows me how dangerous." He muttered. "You...you made her forget."

"I had to." His hands were trembling, although he tried to hide it, and he lifted his chin.

"Thank you for calling today, but I'm afraid I have an appointment I must keep tonight."

A sharp crack sounded where her heart once was. He was sending her away. He was dismissing her. Her gaze fell on his still-trembling hands. He feared her.

"I'm sorry," she said. Her eyes burned and her cheeks heated. Goddess, how humiliating. She checked over both shoulders. Once she confirmed no one was watching, she allowed the shadows to carry her home.

CHAPTER
THIRTEEN

Pierre was a man of logic. When he discovered a new plant or animal, a new event in the heavens that had not yet made it onto his chart, he approached it with fascination. The first time he'd encountered the pawpaw fruit, he'd been enchanted by the plant and delighted when it proved safe to eat. But for every pawpaw he discovered, he'd also come across a foxglove. The plant had proven extremely poisonous and almost killed one of the friars who'd mistaken it for comfrey.

As Isis disappeared into shadow, Pierre thought that she was like foxglove. He'd found her as fascinating as the stars when they'd met, and he was sure her secrets were as infinite. But what he'd witnessed with Allyette told him all he needed to know. She was also poison.

He feared her, not as someone feared the alligator in the swamp. She'd never struck out at him with her magic, and her munitions were not designed to shred or kill. No, what he realized today, was that Isis was dangerous in the way of a sickness, as lethal as a case of consumption. Something invisible that he might never see coming. Exposure to her could alter his thinking, cause him to act irrationally. Was there anything more terrifying than not being certain of one's own mind?

Pierre had nothing if not his own thoughts. The idea that she might tinker with his inner workings, lift ideas from his head and make them disappear, was horrifying and something he never wanted to experience. Still, his chest ached at the thought of not seeing her again. He'd never tell her secret. He admired her too much for that. He rubbed the space over his heart as the immediate shock of what she'd done began to wear off.

Did he actually think Isis would tamper with his mind or any mind if there weren't lives at stake? *No.* He sighed. So what exactly was it about the situation that had left him terrified and resolved to push her away?

"Your friend has gone?" Allyette asked, arriving with the tea.

"Yes." He gestured toward the table. "I will take it alone."

"But she left... in this?" Thunder and lightning cracked nearby, and the woman stared, perplexed, toward the windows.

"She insisted, but not to worry, she didn't have far to go, and she's a supremely resourceful woman."

Allyette placed the tray on the table. "If you say so." She gave a shallow bow and disappeared in the direction of the kitchen.

Pierre drank his tea and waited for the storm to pass. If Isis was dangerous in an innocuous way, it seemed Delphine was an outright menace. If what Isis said was true, Delphine had killed twice now, and he felt a moral obligation to keep that from happening again. He watched the rain through his front windows. Whatever happened with Isis, he needed to do something about Delphine.

Once the rain had stopped, he left the house in search of Étienne. The governor needed to be aware of what was going on. Oh, Pierre was smart enough to know that Étienne would never believe the woman to be a vampire, but she could be placed under suspicion, nonetheless. A few choice words to the right people and she'd be taken care of. He'd make sure of it.

Twilight had fallen on the square, and Pierre's boots squelched in the muddy road as he made his way to the governor's door, the only light coming from the occasional lantern. A prickle traveled along his spine on the dark street. Someone was watching him, following him. He spun, searching the shadows. *Isis?* She could blend into the darkness. It was a possibility. But he didn't call out to her, just walked faster toward the governor's home.

Étienne's servant showed him to a seat by a small fire and went to fetch the governor, who arrived only a moment later, dressed in a long nightshirt and robe. "Monsieur Baron, to what do I owe the pleasure? After the storm tonight, I did not expect to have guests." He gestured to his appearance.

"I apologize for coming without notice, but it's important."

Étienne sank into the chair on the other side of the fire. "Go on."

"I... learned something today. Lucienne, the wife of monsieur Cavalier, who was drained of blood two days ago, she is the sister of Delphine Devereaux Laurent."

Étienne's brow puckered. "The wife of the first victim?"

"Yes."

"Hmmm. That is a coincidence."

111

"I saw Delphine at Touze's the very night after her husband's death, consorting with other men." The lie rolled off Pierre's tongue easily. Although he hadn't seen Delphine himself, he trusted that what Isis had said was true.

The governor scowled as if the thought made him sick. "You think she's responsible."

"We both know that Guillaume was likely not gentle with her. And Lucienne was covered in bruises. I have to wonder if Delphine found a way out of an uncomfortable situation and then did the same for her sister."

Popping out of his chair, Étienne paced the room. "But how? Surely the woman couldn't have physically done it. Guillaume was twice her size. How did she drain the blood of not one but two men? And where did the blood go?"

Pierre ran a hand through his hair. He had to be cautious with this next bit. "It is far too coincidental that two husbands of two sisters die in such a similar way, such an *unholy* death."

Stroking his chin, Étienne frowned miserably. "Unholy. That's the key, isn't it?" The governor paced the length of the room, growing more agitated. "There is too much evidence to point at anyone but Delphine, and the loss of blood is evidence of demonic involvement. I must talk to Father Raphael about this. If there is a witch among us, he will know how to deal with the woman."

Internally, Pierre cheered as the man took the bait. It was only a matter of time now until Delphine was dealt with and the parish was safe again. With a nod of appreciation, Pierre stood from the comfort of the fire. "I was confident you would know what to do, and I'm not disappointed."

The men said their goodbyes, and Pierre strode back out into the street, heading for home. It was late and he was alone, but still, the feeling of being watched lingered. The length of his spine tingled with it, the feeling growing stronger. Was his pursuer closing in? Hell, if it was Isis, he needed to apologize. He'd pushed her away far too abruptly and assumed the worst of her. Yes, he feared what she'd done, but he'd been rash about the whole thing, and he needed to tell her as much.

Drawing a deep breath, he stopped within a weak pool of light cast from a street lantern and squinted into the darkness. "Isis?" he whispered loudly. "Are you there?"

Two glowing yellow eyes cut the darkness and then a woman stepped into view, but it was not Isis. Delphine Devereaux smiled at him, her appearance transformed from the last time he'd seen her, from lovely to otherworldly. Her skin was pale and abnormally smooth, red-painted lips stark against her fair complexion. Tucked into a dress of crimson velvet, dark curls piled effortlessly atop her head, she didn't so much walk toward him as floated, her body moving unnaturally, weightlessly.

"Not Isis, I'm afraid," she said. "Although we share a mutual friend. More my friend than hers these days."

"Delphine?"

"Monsieur Baron, I'm so glad you're here." She flashed him a wicked smile. "You see, my sister is ill, and I think you can help her."

Some part of his logical mind still wanted to reject what she was. How he longed to go back to a time when he could convince himself she was a normal woman. But another part of him, the part that retained ancient and untamed instincts, squirmed in discomfort at her proximity. His every cell screamed *vampire*. He'd believed Isis when she'd suggested as much, but this was different. He felt Delphine's demon nature viscerally, as if he were staring at rotting flesh and not a woman who was so perfect she might have been carved from marble. Beautiful but wrong. Deadly. Repulsive. He took a step back.

"Have you taken her to see Dr. Viel? He'll be able to help her." Pierre took another step away from her, knowing that what Delphine wanted was not anything Viel could deliver, but desperately trying to distract her.

"Don't sell yourself short, Pierre. I think you're exactly what she needs."

Seized from behind, Pierre turned to see the hands on his chest belonged to Lucienne, who'd attacked while he'd been distracted with Delphine. He struggled against her grip, but his efforts were in vain. Her strength was uncanny. Unlike Delphine, she *looked* sickly, her hair caked with filth, her skin hanging from her bones, but somehow, her arms were as solid as any man's. Stronger even. He turned back to Delphine, whose eyes bled from gold to bright red as her teeth extended into fangs.

"Relax, Pierre, and take it like a *man*." She closed in as Lucienne's teeth sank into his neck.

I sis mopped her tears and felt like a foolish child. Alone in her room, she wept over the way Pierre had dismissed her and the fear she'd seen in his eyes. Her heart was broken, and she couldn't even lean on her sisters for support. No way could she reveal to Medea all the things she'd shared with Pierre. She'd performed magic in his presence multiple times. She'd told him everything.

And she didn't regret it.

The truth was, she was falling in love with the man. Desperately, she prayed to the goddess that he'd come to understand what she'd done to Allyette was necessary, and that he'd see her again.

Between her sobs, she could almost hear his voice crying out to her. She dabbed her eyes again, then held her breath, turning toward the mirror in the corner of her room. That was his voice! Pierre was in trouble!

She raced to the looking glass, the image of Pierre in the clutches of the Devereaux sisters revealing itself to her. "Oh Hades, no!"

With a twist of her wand, she called the shadows and

materialized behind Delphine. She had to catch her breath. Lucienne's mouth sucked at Pierre's neck, his body pale and limp in her arms, as Delphine lapped from the same bite, catching the blood that her sister spilled.

"*Ekdioko*," Isis bellowed, casting silver light at Pierre's body. The resulting blast flung Delphine and Lucienne away from him as if by a mighty wind. Isis rushed forward and caught Pierre in her arms, immediately casting a protective ward around them. He was pale, so frightfully pale, but she noticed with no small relief that he was still breathing.

"Pierre? Say something!" She tapped his cheek with her palm, but his head only rolled to the side.

"You might as well feed the rest of him to us, witch," Delphine said, hovering outside the protective ward that shimmered purple in a dome around them. "He's too far gone. He'll never survive."

Isis locked eyes with the woman. "Why? Why would you do this?"

Delphine scoffed just as Lucienne came into view, her skin glowing with newfound energy. "He spoke of me to the wrong person. I didn't like it." She bared her fangs, and Isis cringed. "Did you think you were the only creature deserving of a life here? The only one who wants something better for herself and her family? I know you didn't respect me as an equal when I was human, but if you know what's good for you, you will now."

"Pierre? Pierre?" She ran her fingers through his hair and over his face. He was so cold.

Delphine chuckled. "Don't act like you care about the blood bag. The gods don't worry about the plight of the ants, Isis."

Clutching Pierre, Isis gnashed her teeth at Delphine and

Lucienne. "What do you know of being a goddess? As far as I can see, you are nothing but a devil, a damned demon!"

"That's rich, coming from you."

Isis glared at Delphine, willing her to explain.

The vampire laughed, long and wicked. "I suppose I should thank you for sending Asmodeus my way after he visited us both the night we met on that ship. Those red eyes in the darkness. He came straight to me when you cast him aside, and I was more than happy to meet his needs."

Sharp realization speared her chest and twisted. "Asmodeus made you what you are."

Delphine sneered. "Silence! You don't deserve to say his name. Yes, I owe what I am to my dark love."

"Goddess, Delphine. Can't you see he's made you a monster? Asmodeus is a prince of hell!"

"You shall not speak his name!" Lucienne hissed.

Delphine tapped on the ward with her nail. "We are all monsters, witch. It's only a matter of who has the sharpest teeth." She drew her hand back and scratched at the ward.

Isis yelped with pain as she felt the vampire's claws rip across her shoulder, although her nails never actually touched her. Three bloody tears appeared in her dress. Cursed, demon magic. Delphine couldn't pass through her ward, but her magic could.

Eyes widening, Isis called the shadows to her, shuddering as Delphine pulled back her clawed hand again. Gathering Pierre's considerable weight into her arms, she grunted with the effort, but she had to get Pierre to Rhys. He was her only hope of saving Pierre, whose breath had started to rattle in his lungs.

She howled and strained, folding into shadow and carrying Pierre the considerable distance to Tanglewood Plantation. She made it only as far as the front lawn.

"Rhys! Medea! Someone help me!" she cried.

Rhys appeared in the door to the big house and raced to her side. "Goddess, you're bleeding!"

"Don't worry about me! Him! You must save him," Isis pleaded, rocking Pierre's body in her arms. Was he still breathing? He felt cold.

Medea appeared in front of her. "Isis, what happened?"

"Help her into my office," Rhys commanded, prying Pierre from her grip and lifting him into his arms.

Medea looked between Isis and Pierre, and for a moment, Isis feared she'd argue, but then Medea's gaze focused on her bloody shoulder and her expression softened. "Come, sister. Let's clean you up and save your human."

"SIT DOWN, ISIS. PIERRE IS IN GOOD HANDS, AND SO ARE YOU." Medea frowned down at her as she dabbed a rag soaked in witch hazel to her open wounds.

"He was so cold. I have to know he's all right." Isis tried to get up again, and Medea pushed her back down into the chair.

"These cuts are singed around the edges. They are going to be hell to heal."

Lifting her eyes to her sister's, Isis tried to tamp down her panic. "That's because they were made with demon magic."

"Demons? I thought we were dealing with a vampire."

She shook her head, guilt and pain flooding her. When she spoke again, her voice came out thin as a spider's web. "There's something I have to tell you, and I think you should sit down."

"You talk, I'm going to try a healing spell. I don't like how this looks."

Isis hesitated but decided her confession couldn't wait. "When I...resurrected you, a demon helped me do it."

Medea stopped moving, looked her in the face as if checking that she was serious, and then sat down in the chair across from her. "Go on."

"Asmodeus, the demon of lust."

"One of the princes of hell," Medea clarified.

"Yes. I didn't specifically call on him to help me, but we both command shadows and I had to pass your soul through his dimension to bring you home. He allowed it."

Medea's eyes looked watery as she nodded.

"I'm so sorry, Medea, about what happened to Phineas. Truly, I am."

Her sister ran her hands over her face. "It wasn't your fault, and I have already forgiven you. Tell me what this demon has to do with what happened tonight."

Forgiveness was a balm for a wound that had festered on her soul for a long time, and Isis's shoulders sank with relief. She'd needed to hear that. Although she thought her sister had forgiven her before, time had passed, and they all had more clarity about things and the events of the past. Knowing she forgave her now, after everything, was paramount.

"Asmodeus allowed me to pass through his dimension because he..." Isis swallowed, heat flooding her cheeks. "He fancied me."

Blinking steadily, Medea took her sister's hands. "How do you know this?"

"He propositioned me in my dreams. He promised me power in exchange for becoming one of his brides. I turned him down, and he told me he would never allow me to pass through his dimension again. What I did for you, I will never be able to do for anyone else." Her eyes burned with unshed tears.

"And now he's here, feeding on a human man to torment you?"

Isis's brows shot up. "Oh no. It was Delphine Devereaux, but she told me that she'd dreamed about Asmodeus as well, after I'd rejected him. We met on the ship from Haiti, waking from very similar dreams. Where I said no to Asmodeus, Delphine admitted tonight that she said yes."

Medea scowled. "But she was not even a witch, was she? How was she able to dream walk into his domain?"

"I'm not sure, but my fear is it was because of me."

"You take too much on yourself. No one is responsible for another's dreams."

"The shadows were restless that night on the ship, Medea. What if, somehow, her soul was pulled under with mine? What if I brought her with me into his realm? I know it's not my fault, but I can think of no other explanation."

Medea contemplated this for a moment as she used her wand to magically stitch Isis's wounds. The spell was working, and Isis noticed an immediate reduction in pain. "It's possible, but it will do no good to dwell on what's done. However it happened, there is no doubt that Delphine is now a vampiric creature drunk on demon magic. She is his bride and responsible for two murders."

"Yes. And she's brought in Lucienne, her sister. There is another sister...Antoinette. I saw them all together. I am certain they plan to turn her as well."

"Why do you think they targeted Pierre?"

Isis released a heavy sigh. "Delphine said he spoke ill of her to someone. I don't know the details."

Medea finished with her wounds and handed her a small glass of healing elixir. "Why was he out at that hour and so soon after the storm?"

Throwing back the elixir, she returned the glass to her sister. "I have no idea."

Just then, Rhys's voice cut through the room. "Circe! Goddess!"

They ran into his office to find the walls crawling with twining ivy. It spiraled around and reached across every surface of the room, crossing Pierre's legs where he lay unconscious on Rhys's examination table.

Circe and Rhys stood near his desk, water gushing from between Circe's legs. Their sister looked them straight in the eyes and simply said, "It's time."

"She's in labor," Rhys said dumbly, as if it wasn't obvious. The poor man was clearly stunned.

"*Fuck!*" Medea raced to Circe's side, supporting her as another contraction hit and a paperweight on Rhys's desk transformed into a sparrow and flew across the room.

Torn between helping her sister and helping Pierre, who was swiftly becoming grown over with ivy, Isis froze. Thankfully, Rhys snapped out of his stupor and into his role as a healer.

"Get him out of here, Isis. Put him in one of the bedrooms. He's stable. He just needs time to rest. We need the office to deliver the baby."

Isis nodded, then sent a bright silver spell barreling into the ivy wrapped around Pierre. The vines snapped, and she rushed in, pulling him into her arms. She called the shadows to her, grateful they didn't have far to go this time because she had very little power left.

Everything went dark, and then she was in her room, laying him on her bed and tucking him in. He was still pale, but his lashes fluttered as she adjusted his head on the pillow.

"Isis," he said weakly.

She squeezed his shoulder. "You're safe now."

"I'm sorry. I... I..."

She kissed his forehead. "Shh. I have to go. There's something I have to do. Rest now."

CHAPTER
FIFTEEN

Without the energy to travel by shadow again, Isis ran back to the office the old-fashioned way to find the ivy had bloomed, and Rhys and Medea were sneezing and coughing against the thick pollen filling the air.

"Isis! Thank the goddess! Can you open the window? I can't breathe in here," Medea said.

Isis turned the lever and pushed the window open, enjoying a full breath of night air. A sparrow darted outside over her head.

At least they had managed to get Circe out of her dress and onto the table, where she rested under a thin blanket.

"Sooorry," Circe said, rubbing her belly. "I can't control it. It happens every time I—" She screamed and gripped her belly as another contraction consumed her, and a fire ignited in the middle of the room. Isis stomped it out.

"They're coming closer together," Medea cried.

Rhys agreed and positioned his wife's legs so he could take a look. "Coming fast. I can see the head. The next contraction, I need you to push."

Hurrying to her sister's side, Isis took Circe's hand just as another contraction crashed into her, and the floor shook. Shoots sprouted between the planks of the floor, growing from saplings to fully grown trees that tested the ceiling in minutes. Butterflies popped into existence, fluttering around her head, and ferns spread their leaves against her legs.

Circe's earsplitting scream had Isis gripping her hand even tighter. And then Rhys was pulling the babe out. The child was surrounded by twinkling lights and the sounds of birds who sang with joy from the trees that now monopolized the room.

"Who is it?" Circe asked her husband. "Endora or Percival?"

Isis couldn't see what Rhys was doing at the end of the table until he stood up with the baby wrapped in a blanket in his arms. He rounded the table and handed the bundle to his wife. "Endora. It's a girl!"

Squealing with delight, Isis gently kissed the side of Circe's head. "Congratulations."

Medea beamed the largest smile Isis had ever seen on her face. Remarkable. Medea could have been jealous or triggered by this birth, but she looked invigorated, as if the arrival of her niece meant everything. Their eyes met over their sister.

"A girl!" Medea repeated, her voice full of wonder.

Isis looked down at the tiny witch. She was no bigger than a large cat, with eyes the color of deep water just like her mother's and a shock of black hair closer to Rhys's color. Endora blinked up at her, mouth forming a perfect "O" as her tiny fingers worked along the edge of the blanket. Isis hooked one finger into that tiny hand and was surprised when Endora squeezed. Love sparked in Isis's chest, for her sisters, the new baby, and the family they'd made here.

"She's so beautiful, Circe. Perfect," Isis said.

"I agree," Medea added.

"Of course, she's a Tanglewood," Rhys said, kissing Circe on the lips.

Circe brought the babe to her breast, and a flock of brightly colored birds flapped from the trees, circled the room, and then flew out the window.

"Soooorry," Circe said, eyeing the trees. Spanish moss had appeared in the branches. Isis could no longer make out any part of the room. It looked like she'd given birth in the middle of the rain forest.

Rhys stroked her hair. "Don't worry about a thing, Circe. We'll have this all cleaned up by morning."

One by one, they gripped one another's hands, surrounding Circe and Endora, and basking in the magic of family.

PIERRE WOKE IN A ROOM THAT WAS NOT HIS OWN TO THE SOUND of... parrots. It took him a moment to remember that Isis had brought him here after saving him from—by God, Delphine was a vampire and her sister too! His hand went to his neck, where a bandage covered the two wounds there.

Another squawk came from the corner of the room, and he narrowed his eyes at the two birds that didn't belong. That genus and species had no business being in Louisiana. He only knew what they were from his studies and the unusual menagerie a colleague housed in Paris. But then, he was in the house of a witch. He supposed anything was possible.

He leaned back against the pillows and took the opportunity to peruse the room, Isis's room. The furnishings were simple but functional, a four-poster bed, a dresser, a woven rug, and in the corner, a mirror. The silver glinted in the light from the window. Wait, that wasn't right. It was evening. Nighttime. Outside, the moon shone barely a sliver on the horizon, surrounded by nothing but darkness and stars. Inside, there were candles, but none positioned properly to be the cause of the glimmer.

So what was the mirror reflecting?

He tossed back the covers and carefully lowered his feet over the side of the bed. His head pounded hard enough to rival a drum corps, and as he rose to standing, the room wavered like a boat at sea. Slowly, bracing himself on the bed, he hobbled toward the stretch of silver. But when he gazed into its depths, all he saw was his own reflection.

He looked like the dead. Pale, eyes bloodshot, mud in his hair. He ran his hands through it, righting it as much as possible. Working his fingers beneath the dressing on his neck, he loosened it, then tugged it down to reveal two puncture wounds, exactly the same as the ones he'd seen on the two dead men. Delphine Devereaux was a vampire and so was her sister, and they'd targeted him! If not for Isis, he'd be dead, bloodless, abandoned in the street.

Step by careful step, he made it to the door. As soon as he opened it, the colorful birds he'd seen earlier flew overhead and soared down a set of stairs at the end of a hall. Rubbing his temples, he followed after them.

When Isis had put him to bed, she'd removed his shoes and stockings. Pierre hadn't thought much of it until he stepped off the bottom step and the wet carpet squelched between his toes like moss after a rain. No, as he peered down at the floor through squinted eyes, he confirmed it was, in fact, moss he was standing on. "What in the bloody hell?"

He had to be dreaming. That was the only explanation for this. To his left, a tree grew right through the middle of the house. He traced his gaze up its trunk and found the two parrots resting in a branch near the hole in the ceiling. Did he have a fever? He pressed a hand to his head. He didn't feel hot.

Voices floated from a room to his right, and he padded toward them, gait uneven, bracing himself on anything he could reach. He stopped in the doorway, both hands gripping the doorjamb on either side of his shoulders to hold himself up. The room within had been devoured by a forest, deep green and blooming with every manner of flower. Bees buzzed. Butterflies flitted. Birds soared. He blinked at the vines, the trees, the bushes. The botanist in him wanted to study it all. The rest of him couldn't get his head around what he was seeing.

At the center of the room, he found his Isis. Why had he thought it that way? Was she his? That was to be determined. Beside her, a woman who must have been her sister based on resemblance lay in a narrow bed with a babe in her arms. Medea and a man he'd never met stood on the mother's other side.

He cleared his throat, and all four heads turned to stare at him.

"Pierre! What are you doing out of bed?" Isis held out her hands and started picking her way through the underbrush to get to him.

"You—" His voice cut out on a rasp, his tongue as dry as

a strap of leather. He cleared his throat and tried again. "You have a jungle in your house."

Isis reached him and wrapped an arm around his waist for support. "Yes, but don't be alarmed. This isn't something that happens every day."

A laugh exploded from his chest. "Not every day, you say? That's a relief." He couldn't stop laughing and was relieved when Isis's chuckle joined his own.

"It happened because the baby was born," Isis said. "It will go back to normal in a day or two."

He turned his head to look at her. God, she was beautiful. No woman had ever fascinated Pierre as much as Isis. Part of him noted again that he should be afraid, but for some reason, the fear was far away again, impersonal. Nothing about tonight was normal. Nothing about this woman was normal. But when he looked at Isis, all he saw was a miracle of nature, a discovery of paradise he never wanted to leave, a gift woven for him by the universe. Or maybe it was the other way around. Maybe he'd been created for her.

Why wasn't he afraid? "Do I have a fever?" he asked, swaying against her.

She placed a hand on his forehead. "I don't think so, but you lost a lot of blood tonight."

Pierre blinked. "You're so beautiful, Isis. Stunning. Any man would count himself lucky to be with you." He shifted unsteadily in her arms, and she grunted with the effort to right him.

"You need to rest. Let's get you back to bed," she said softly.

He didn't move, just stared at her, losing himself in the deep blue of her eyes, so similar to that of the night sky right after the sun set. What universes must exist inside this woman, waiting to be discovered? If she were his, he'd never tire of her. If she were his... *He should make her his.*

She tried to guide him toward the stairs, but he planted his heels. "Pierre, you'll have to move your feet. I'm far too exhausted to carry you up the stairs."

"Marry me," he blurted. Had he just said that out loud? Yes, he had, and he did not regret it. At the look of surprise on her face, he repeated himself. "Marry me, Isis."

"The man is babbling," her sister Medea said from the door to the forest. "Put him in the salon and give him some whiskey to settle his nerves. You'll never make it up the stairs with him."

"I'm not babbling or confused or feverish," he said loudly. He faltered in her arms and caught himself on the wall. "Okay, the current state of things isn't exactly optimal, but that doesn't mean I don't know what I'm saying. My mind is perfectly clear. Maybe the clearest it's ever been. I see my future and know what's missing. You. You are the woman for me, Isis. I must have you. I want to be the one to give you everything."

Isis stared at him, her smile growing, and a wonderful lightness in his chest told him she was going to say yes. But before the word left her lips, lightning flashed. She yelled something foul, and then there was nothing but darkness.

CHAPTER
SIXTEEN

"**M**edea! He's already unwell from blood loss. Did you have to knock him out?" Isis glared at her sister.

"Relax. It's a simple sleeping charm that will wear off in a matter of minutes. He was delusional." Medea raised her chin as if she saw no problem with her behavior.

"Can you two take it outside?" Circe growled from her spot on the table. She kissed the top of Endora's head. "I don't want the negativity around the new baby."

Rhys gave them both a look sharp enough to cut.

Medea strode to Isis's side before pointing her wand over her shoulder and muttering a short incantation. Tree branches moved aside, and the door to the office closed gently, a shimmy of purple signifying she'd blocked the sound.

"Why?" Isis insisted, pointing both hands at Pierre.

"I saw what was happening," Medea said. "You almost said yes to him."

Isis's head grew hot. "That was the point. It was a marriage proposal. I *would* have said yes!"

The expression on Media's face morphed into pure outrage. "Have you lost your mind? He's a human."

"So are we." She shrugged.

"We are witches, a very specific and magical species of human. He is an earth human. No magic. Terrible tempers. May I remind you that his kind burns people they think are witches, Isis? They burn their own women under suspicion of being *us*."

Hot anger built in her veins, and Isis turned on her sister. "Pierre would never do that to anyone, especially not us."

"You don't know that." Medea rolled her eyes.

"I do know it. He knows what I am, and he's told no one. He loves me, Medea. And, you know..." Isis paused to examine her feelings. She hadn't known Pierre long, but when she'd seen him in Lucienne's arms tonight, the emotions that raged in her had one thing in common. Whether it was the initial jealousy of seeing the woman's lips on his neck, the resulting anger, or the terror that he might die, the root of all those emotions was a feeling of possessiveness. Pierre was hers and hers alone. "I love him too."

Medea's eyes turned glossy. "I forbid it."

"Why? Am I not allowed love and happiness?"

"No, you're not!" Medea snapped.

Isis trembled at her sister's words. There was so much bitterness in her tone. So much anger. "Why would you say such a terrible thing?" When Medea didn't answer, Isis stared at her, willing her to explain herself. All she saw was a shadow that passed through her sister's expression tinged with guilt. "Goddess, you don't want me to find love because you're afraid of being alone."

"I didn't say that." Medea looked down at her wand gripped between her fingers.

"You had years with Tavyss. You had love, Medea, true love."

"And now I have nothing."

Isis shuffled back. "And you'd rather I never experience love than remind you of what you had?"

Medea waved a hand dismissively. "Remind me? I don't need to be reminded, Isis. I think about Tavyss and Phineas every minute of every single day." Her voice cracked. "And you wonder why I don't think it's wise for you to take a fragile human as your husband? Do you think I would enjoy watching you go through the same thing I did?"

"That won't happen. I can protect him. Rhys can heal him. I have as much of a chance of growing old with him as I would with a witch."

"And then what? Do you plan to have children with the man?"

"Maybe."

Medea harrumphed and looked away from her.

"What is this really about, Medea? I don't believe you'd deprive me of a man I loved simply to save me from a possible future where he dies before I do. The three of us have been around a long time. We don't age like the humans here or even the witches of Darnuith. We were born in the Garden of the Hesperides and have a tree that roots us to that immortal power. Have you ever considered that Rhys will likely go before Circe too? If you insist we insulate ourselves from any future hurt, you deny us any relationships aside from each other."

Her sister's eyes grew wet with tears. "I've already been sentenced to that fate."

Isis balked at the admission, watching Medea's walls crumble and vulnerability show in her slumped shoulders. Across Pierre's sleeping body, Isis pulled Medea into her arms. "I'm not going to leave you alone. You will always have me and Circe and Rhys and little Endora too! You're my sister! I will never remove you from my life, not ever. But you must know that adding Pierre will only grow our family and increase those who truly know and care for you." She took Medea's hands in her own. "I know things have been hard for you since Tavyss and Phineas were murdered. I know you are still grieving what happened, and I don't blame you for resenting me for what I did to you, bringing you back—"

"Did to me? You resurrected me. Who could blame you for that?" Medea looked away, unable to meet her eyes.

"You could blame me. Bringing you back shredded your heart. If we'd left you in the beyond..."

"None of us knows for sure what would have happened. Our power has always come from our connection. You and Circe might have been weakened or lost your powers completely. You might have been captured by Eleanor. I know why you did what you did, Isis, and I don't blame you for my pain, although I can't deny feeling it."

At their feet, Pierre moaned.

Medea sighed heavily. "If you want this man, Isis, and you truly believe in him, you have my blessing. You don't need it to do what you want to do, but I give it to you freely anyway."

Isis pulled her into a firm hug. "Oh, thank you, Medea!"

"Are you strong enough to carry him home? He'll heal better in his own place." Medea cast a soft look at Pierre as Isis gathered him into her arms.

"I will find the strength," Isis said.

"I love you, sister," Medea said. "You must know that all

of this...trouble...I've made for you, it comes from a place of love."

"I know." Isis raised her wand, calling the shadows. "I won't be back tonight."

A ghost of a smile turned Medea's lips, but she remained silent as the night carried Isis and Pierre away.

CHAPTER
SEVENTEEN

P ierre's eyes fluttered open to silvery light. The sun was rising, and he was outside. Yes, there was his telescope and the sky beyond. He was on his terrace. Air wafted across his cheeks, bringing him to his senses. Why was he sleeping on his terrace?

He stood up and cracked his aching back, fabric bunching under his chin. He dug his hands under the dressing and pulled it from his neck. Testing the area with his fingers, he determined the wound had stopped bleeding. He tried to remember the circumstance that had led him here. He'd been with Isis at Tanglewood Plantation, but then what happened?

Turning to go inside, he balked when he noticed her curled in a ball in the shaded corner. He hadn't noticed her there before, but then, she seemed to blend with the shadows, and he wondered if that was part of her magic. Maybe they were hiding her, protecting her. *Putain*! She looked woefully uncomfortable in that position.

"Isis." He squatted beside her and brushed her hair back from her face.

Her lashes fluttered. "Need sleep," she groaned. "Oh, Pierre. Just leave me here. Overused my magic. So tired."

"I see that, *mon étoile*, but this is a terrible place to sleep."

This time, her eyes did fully open, and she grinned up at him. "You called me your star."

"You are. The brightest one in my sky. Now, come. You'll be more comfortable in bed."

She flashed him a wicked grin. "You're taking me to bed? Why, Monsieur Baron, you're positively scandalous."

He pinched her chin. "I wish I was capable of making good on that descriptor, though I'm afraid the spirit is willing, but the flesh is weak. You and I need rest, a hot meal, and a bath, not necessarily in that order."

She arched a brow. "The bath appeals."

"*Mon Dieu*, you're a temptress." He stood, helping her up as he rose.

She stretched herself against him, wrapping her arms around his neck and pressing her lips to his. "*Your* temptress."

He searched her face. "Mine? Truly?"

She nodded enthusiastically. "Yes."

"Will you marry me, Isis?"

Her smile grew. "Yes."

Joy flooded his heart, and he squeezed her to him, lifting her feet in a half twirl. "Very well, then I, too, vote that we start with a bath." Taking her hand, he quietly opened the door and looked right and left down the hall before leading her down the stairs and to his chambers. Thankfully, the house was empty at this hour, too early for even the servants to have begun their daily routines.

Once safely behind closed doors, Pierre lit the candelabra. Only then did he face the reality of the empty copper tub in the corner of the room and the cold fireplace. He'd need to start a fire to heat the water he carried in from the pump. Isis could rest while he managed it.

"What is it?" Isis asked, following his gaze to the tub.

"I'll need to pump the water. Normally, one of the servants would help, but I don't wish to draw attention to your being here, so..."

Isis lifted her chin. "Oh, Pierre, you forget you're marrying a witch." She drew her wand from her sleeve and, with a flourish, filled the tub with steaming water.

He turned to her in delight. "Brilliant!" He touched her wand skeptically, then turned it between his fingers, inspecting it from every angle. "Where does the water come from? Does it come from the inside of this device?"

"No," she chuckled. "It's magic. It's elemental. My power is transforming the air inside the tub into water. Do you want to see me transform it to fire?" She raised her wand, but he grabbed her elbow and lowered it again.

"I'd much rather we enjoy the water." Absently, he scratched the healing wounds on his neck.

"The bite looks better." She reached for the spot, inspecting the lesions. He gloried in the feel of it. Her touch seemed to trail to his toes from the inside, although her fingers never left his neck. "Another day or two and I doubt you'll be able to see it at all."

"Thanks to you." He brushed a knuckle along her jaw. "I'd rather not draw any unwanted attention. You were right about Delphine, and I suspect, by now, Étienne has arrested her and locked her up. No sense confusing the issue with another mark."

Isis froze. "What do you mean, Étienne will be arresting her?"

"I visited with him just before the incident. I told him I

suspected she was... supernatural. She'll be captured and interrogated."

The gasp that rose from Isis's throat disturbed him. "You shouldn't have done that. She heard you, Pierre. That's why she attacked you. She told me as much."

He shrugged. "All the more reason she should be behind bars."

"You don't understand. That will never work."

"Why not?"

"Because I was *wrong* about Delphine being a vampire. She *is* like a vampire in that she drinks blood, but unlike that species, she can tolerate the sun and enjoys additional powers fueled by demonic magic. For one, we know she turned her sister Lucienne to be like her. That's not possible where I come from. Delphine is channeling a demon of the underworld. She can't be burned. No prison will hold her."

Pierre's stomach sank like a stone. "But then, how do we stop her and Lucienne from striking again?"

Isis seemed to ponder this. "We'll have to trap them on holy ground and bind them magically."

He groaned. "Please tell me that's simpler than it sounds." He rubbed his neck wound. "She does have one sister left human."

Deep blue eyes met his. "I'll protect you, Pierre. She can't hurt you as long as we're together, and my sisters and I will find a way to stop them from hurting anyone else."

"You'll protect me." He laughed under his breath. It was not supposed to be this way. Wasn't he, as the man, supposed to protect her? But oddly, he didn't feel threatened by her pronouncement in the least. It would be like feeling threatened by the sun's offer to warm him. She was magic, a goddess, a star. His star.

"Now, about this bath." Shadows leached off the walls and began untying the laces of her dress.

"The shadows follow your commands." Pierre watched in wonder as the darkness undressed her, as careful with the material as any lady's maid.

She stroked her hands along the outside of his arms. "They obey me, yes." His breath hitched as she stepped out of her dress, wearing nothing but a whisper-thin shift that left little to the imagination.

His cock twitched, and his gaze drifted down along her exposed collarbone, over her firm breasts, her taut abdomen, and the dark triangle between her thighs. Oh, how he wanted to explore every part of her. She was a land in need of discovery, and he was the explorer eager to brave her wilds.

He swallowed around a thick tongue. "Tell them I can manage the rest on my own."

"Done," she said softly. The shadows slunk back to the door.

Reaching behind his head, he grabbed the back of his shirt, pulling it off over his head. When her eyes raked over him and turned heated, he didn't hide his satisfaction. Her fingers found his fly, and in minutes, he was naked before her, his cock hard and ready.

Gripping the bottom of her shift, he unveiled her slowly, every luscious curve revealing itself to him inch by glorious inch. He released a shaky breath, unsteady for want of her, but gathered himself quickly. Offering her his hand, he beckoned her toward the tub.

She slipped her fingers into his.

He tested the water, finding it deliciously hot before sinking in and ducking under. She stepped in after but stayed standing for a moment, straddling his legs. Good

God, the sight of her body was kindling, igniting a fire in his blood he'd never thought possible. His gaze raked up her legs, catching on the juncture of her thighs.

"Let me wash your hair." She motioned for him to turn around so that his back was to her. Perching on the edge of the tub, she dug the soap from its dish and started rubbing it between her palms. He closed his eyes against an urge to turn his head and trail kisses up her inner thigh.

"Are you well enough for this?" he asked. "You said on the terrace that you were tired?"

She started scrubbing his hair, her nails working the soap into his scalp. "Surprisingly, all hints of fatigue have left me," she said softly. Her fingers slowed in his hair. "I am nervous, though."

He inhaled sharply at that admission. "I make you nervous, *mon etoile*? Why? I'd think the goddess who commands shadows wouldn't be nervous of anything."

"It's been a long time since I've been with a man, and I've never been with your kind. I'm afraid I won't be what you expect."

At her urging, he tipped his head back, staring up at her between her knees. She cupped water in her hand and rinsed his hair. "It is what I love about you most. Everything about you is unexpected. Mysterious. Exceptional." He turned his head, placing a kiss on her inner thigh.

The delicate gasp she released was all the encouragement he needed. She sank into the water behind him until her face was level with his. Turning, he kissed her then, probing her mouth and stroking her tongue with his own. She groaned in response, opening for him, her mouth accommodating his exploration. Her breasts rested above the surface, and he trailed his wet fingers over one, weighed it in his palm before teasing her nipple into a hard peak with his thumb. Rolling and pinching her nipple between his thumb and finger, he coaxed another gasp from her, devouring the sound with his kiss.

"You like that?" he whispered against her lips. "Then we must try the other." He repositioned himself and then turned her, pulling her back against his chest, her bottom flush against his hard length. He slid his hand, wet and warm, to her other breast, where he repeated the process, watching the results over her shoulder as he whispered in her ear. "You're so beautiful, *mon etoile*. There isn't a star in the sky as bright as you."

He shifted her, grinding his cock against her backside and kneading her breasts with one hand as his other traveled down the slope of her abdomen. She leaned her head back against his shoulder, her eyes hooded and her breath coming in shallow pants. "That feels... Goddess, Pierre. Please."

He drifted his hand lower, and a thrill of anticipation filled him when she arched against him in response, sending water rippling. He gripped her thighs and spread her wider. She obliged until her knees touched the sides of the tub. He returned his hand to the place where her thighs met.

"Tell me what you want, Isis."

"Touch me," she said between pants.

"Touch you where?" He grinned against the side of her cheek, wild with need for her but wanting to hear her say it.

"Between my legs."

He grunted his response and slid his fingers along her slit, then rubbed slow, languid circles around her clit. She moaned and bucked against his hand, and he plucked her nipple, gently pinching the nub between her legs at the same time, noting her enthusiastic response. "*Mon etoile*, let us see if we can make you shine brighter."

He hooked his hand and sank a finger inside her, continuing to circle with his thumb as he pumped in and out, watching her thighs clench beneath the surface. Two fingers and her flesh quaked, her hips finding a rhythm against him, faster, harder, chasing her release.

Moving his other hand from her breast to her throat, he gripped under her jaw, holding her head against his shoulder as he quickened his thrusting fingers. "Burn for me, *petite étoile*."

Her breath caught and her body tensed. Shadows exploded from her. The water rose straight up as her thighs clenched together around his hand and she writhed in his arms. He watched in amazement, desire riding him. The water, the darkness, it all came crashing back into the tub as her body turned boneless against him.

He kissed the side of her head and stroked her hair. "Extraordinary."

Drawing a deep breath into her lungs, she flipped over, kneeling between his legs and turning those deep-water blues on him. "Now, you've surprised me."

He quirked a brow. "About what, specifically?"

"I hadn't thought there was anything about this realm that was better than Ouros, but I was wrong. *That* was better than anything I've ever experienced before, in any dimension."

Hooding his eyes, he lowered his lips to her ear. "*That* isn't over."

CHAPTER
EIGHTEEN

Isis's heart pounded in her chest as she floated over Pierre, still buzzing from the orgasm he'd given her. He was hard and ready, but what she had in store for him couldn't be done in a tub. "Filthy. I know just what to do with a man like you." She straddled his legs and kissed him softly, then grabbed the bar of soap and started lathering his chest and shoulders. He moaned as she kneaded his thighs and then pressed her chest against him to scrub his back.

"*Putain*, Isis, you'll kill me with desire."

Rinsing him clean, she shot him a heated look. "Now, what to do about that filthy mouth and filthy mind?"

He raised his hips, and his substantial length pressed hard between her legs. "I can think of a few things." He leaned in to take her mouth, but she rose from the water and stepped out of the tub, tugging his hand toward the bed.

"Do you want a towel?" he asked, but she didn't stop until his knees hit the edge of the bed and his back slapped the mattress.

"I don't care about getting dry," she said, nudging him to the middle of the massive four-poster. "Or covering up."

He combed his fingers through his wet locks and nested them behind his head, his cock jutting out toward her in all its glory. "What do you want now, *mon etoile*?" His lips turned up in a wolfish grin.

"Keep your eyes on me," she commanded. Prowling up his legs, she lowered her mouth to his cock.

The sound Pierre made was nothing short of carnal as she sucked him to the back of her throat, delighting in the power she had to give him pleasure. It was one thing to have magical power. Quite another to wield the power of a woman over a man, body and soul. That's what he was giving her. The adoration in his eyes was nothing short of worship.

"I need to be in you," he murmured, grabbing her shoulders and drawing her up to kiss her again. When she straddled his hips, he flipped her over. His mouth crashed down on hers again as his cock nudged her entrance. Ever so slowly, he pushed in, stretching her to her limit. She hadn't been with a lover in years and never someone like Pierre. He coupled their hands on either side of her head and locked eyes with her, burying himself to the hilt. She couldn't muffle the moan of pleasure that escaped her lips.

And then he was moving, his body stroking inside hers at the same time his mouth did sinful things to her tongue, her neck. Her pleasure drew the shadows again. They brushed around Pierre, tousling his hair before sweeping along his spine, between his legs.

"Isis, my God..." He pounded into her in earnest, and her body spilled over into pleasure like an overflowing goblet. She writhed under him, then shattered, rocking against his hips as he followed her into oblivion. They remained tangled in each other, skin damp from both exertion and their bath.

He stroked her hair back from her face. "*Je t'aime, mon étoile.*"

She kissed him solidly. "I love you too. So much, it makes my heart ache."

"Come with me to see the priest now. We can be married this afternoon." He pressed his forehead to hers.

"Why the rush?" She giggled.

He gripped her hands between their chests. "For one, we took no precautions. You might be carrying our child even now."

The thought made something powerful blossom inside her heart, soft petals opening. "I'm pleased the thought of my being with child doesn't frighten you, but I can stop that from happening with a simple potion. We don't have to rush."

He kissed her on the nose, then bounded off the bed and started to dress. "Oh, I intend to rush. I aim to make this permanent before you come to your senses and change your mind about me."

She laughed, leaning back on her elbows to watch him. "I'm not going to change my mind."

"Then I must marry you so that you can spend every night in my bed without excuse or need for stealth. I want you on my arm and by my side always."

Fetching her dress, she hailed the shadows to help her back on with it. "Very well, we'll go to see him after breakfast. Have Allyette make us something. I'm about to arrive at your front door." She circled her wand, and the shadows carried her outside the wall.

After lingering over breakfast to the raised eyebrows of Pierre's servants, not because they suspected she'd spent the night—she made sure to appear as if she'd arrived by invitation at the gate—but because their lingering stares made their affection for each other as apparent as anything could be, Isis accompanied Pierre to the parish church, where their engagement was posted in the wedding banns. The priest agreed to marry them in three weeks' time, an eternity for Isis, who had no intention of keeping her hands off him for that long.

"You'll just have to stay at Tanglewood Plantation," she insisted as they strolled the square that evening.

He grinned. "You'll ruin me, mademoiselle. You'll start a scandal."

She laughed. "Three weeks, Pierre. No doubt, I will see you in my dreams. I suspect the night itself will round you up and bring you to me."

With a wink, he brushed his hand along her arm, awakening fire in her blood once more. "Who am I to deny the night itself?"

Leaning into him, she was surprised when he stopped short and whispered in her ear, "Be alert. Blakemore is coming. Strange man. Not someone to give any reason for scrutiny."

Isis followed his gaze to see the dragon himself, Gabriel Blakemore, headed straight for them, a square of parchment in his hands. "The purveyor of imported goods? I thought he was the type to keep to himself."

"Oh, he is," Pierre murmured. "But that's the problem. On the rare occasion he does speak, everyone listens. There's not a soul in this parish that doesn't fear getting on his wrong side."

The twitch of Gabriel's lips told her the dragon had

heard every word, but he didn't admit to it as he approached them and bowed slightly at the waist. "Monsieur Baron. Mademoiselle Tanglewood."

"Good to see you again, Blakemore." Pierre gave him a formal smile, his hand subtly pressing possessively into her fingers on his arm as if he were afraid if he let go, Isis would float directly into Gabriel's arms. Little did he know just how unlikely that would be. Aside from Tavyss and Medea, she was not aware of a single dragon/witch pairing. The relationship was exceedingly rare and now prohibited in Paragon.

"I heard congratulations are in order." Gabriel smiled, his dark eyes flashing with internal fire.

Now, Pierre preened. "*Oui.* I've worn her down, and she's agreed to become my wife."

Isis laughed. "I'm not sure who wore who down, but yes, we will be wed."

"Excellent." Gabriel's gaze met hers. "In that case, I'm sure you'll only need one of these, but perhaps, Isis, you can deliver the other one to your sisters." He handed a rectangular envelope to Pierre and another to Isis.

She untied the ribbon holding the invitation shut and unfolded the corners. "You're holding a masquerade?"

The dragon tipped his head in acknowledgment. "Tomorrow night. My first. I think it's time we all got to know one another better, especially considering recent events."

"You mean the murders," Pierre clarified.

"And the capture of the murderer." Gabriel fixed her with an intense stare. "The killer was arrested just this morning. Delphine Devereaux. They say she murdered her husband and then her sister's husband."

Isis gripped Pierre's arm tighter. "They caught her?"

149

Gabriel leveled a loaded stare. "Only an hour ago. They've imprisoned her, awaiting trial."

Isis shot a look at Pierre, her eyes widening. This was what she was afraid of. No wonder the dragon was throwing this masquerade on short notice. Gabriel knew exactly what it meant that Delphine was in prison, and he was creating an alibi. Isis gripped her invitation tighter.

"Now, if you'll excuse me, I have a few more invitations to extend." Gabriel bowed and then strode away.

Pierre waited until he thought Gabriel was out of earshot before whispering, "I thought you said no prison could hold her."

"It can't," Isis said. "But if she breaks free, she shows the humans what she is. I suspect Delphine is smarter than that. She's likely, even now, conspiring to prove her innocence."

"Do you mean..." Pierre tipped his head back and stared at the sky. "Lucienne."

Isis sighed. "Will likely strike again while her sister is locked up, proving Delphine isn't the murderer."

CHAPTER
NINETEEN

Back at Tanglewood Plantation, Isis brought her sisters up-to-date on the day's events, while Pierre returned home to manage his work responsibilities.

"The dragon invited all of us?" Circe asked, Endora nestled in her arms, while Rhys perched on the arm of the chair beside her. The rain forest in Rhys's office had begun to recede, but the occasional parrot soared through the room with a resounding squawk. "An actual ball! I haven't been to a proper masquerade since we left Darnuith."

Medea crossed her arms. "Did you miss the part where Isis announced she's engaged to be married, Circe? I think that is far more exciting news."

Circe shrugged. "Of course she's engaged! Anyone can see she loves Pierre, and he thinks this planet's single sun rises from her ass."

Rhys chuckled and kissed his wife's cheek. "What my wife is so colorfully trying to say is congratulations, Isis. We hope Pierre makes you as happy as we are."

"Now, can we talk about this ball?" Circe asked excitedly.

"No," Isis insisted. "We need to talk about Delphine. It's safe to assume she's conspiring to have herself freed. If she left prison by magical means, people would know what she was. She needs to prove her innocence, which means arranging a murder while she's locked up. It's likely Lucienne will strike again sometime soon."

Medea heaved a beleaguered sigh. "Beginning immediately, make sure your time is accounted for. The demon would likely love to pin this on one of us—or Pierre, as the man who turned her in. Don't give her the opportunity."

"Even more reason to go to the ball," Circe said. "To see and be seen. Please say we're going. I feel cooped up in this house."

Rhys was quick to voice his support. "Leave Endora with me and go with your sisters. We'll be safe behind the wards, and the three of you will be accounted for."

Circe squealed excitedly. "I wonder if there will be dancing. I love dancing." She gazed up at her husband with so much love on her face, it made Isis's heart swell in her chest.

"For the love of the goddess," Medea said. "The lot of you are enough to rot my teeth with how sweet you are toward each other. *I'll* watch Endora. You'll both go to the ball."

Truly?" Circe beamed.

Medea rolled her eyes. "Yes. No part of me wants to spend the evening watching you and Isis hang off your romantic partners. Leave me a quiet house, a book, and this little darling, and go have a good time. And make yourselves seen."

Isis wrapped her arms around Medea's shoulders and hugged. "You are the best sister."

She grunted. "For goddess's sake, take care of one

another. Demon magic is dangerous, and when it came to Pierre, Delphine enjoyed toying with you at his expense far too much. That prison can't hold her if she wants out, and we all know Lucienne is just as dangerous. Keep an eye on her."

"I'll keep Pierre safe," Isis said. "Besides, I doubt Gabriel will allow supernatural mischief at his ball. He's guarded his secret too closely for that. Based on the look he gave me when he invited us, absolutely nothing about our current situation has escaped his attention."

"I'VE NEVER SEEN A MORE BEAUTIFUL WOMAN." PIERRE BOWED TO kiss Isis's hand. She'd appeared in the shadows around the corner from Blakemore's at precisely eight o'clock as planned, dressed in a gown of rich lapis blue that brought out her eyes and made his inner workings heat with desire. He lowered his mouth to her ear and whispered, "You are stunning in that dress, but I'd prefer to see you out of it. Are you sure we can't skip the ball and go straight to bed?"

She pulled away, laughing. "My sister would never allow it. She's been looking forward to this all day."

"What have I been looking forward to?" Circe, in a rose-colored dress trimmed in white lace, sidled up to them, her mask dangling from her fingers.

"This ball. I'd be willing to bet you'll combust into a heap of ashes if we delay much longer."

Rhys stroked his beard. "Isis is right. My best estimate is that we have less than ten minutes until detonation."

Although Pierre didn't know Circe and Rhys like he knew Isis, he felt at home with them almost immediately.

The easy way they teased each other spoke to a deep bond he longed to be a part of.

"*Non*, I can't have you exploding. As I am the architect and engineer of this parish, you'll make too much work for me."

He was pleased when they chuckled at his teasing. One by one, they tied on their masks and then rounded the corner to the event. People filed in the front doors of the grand home that was adjacent to Blakemore's Imports. Pierre offered Isis his arm and led her inside, where a servant presented them with a tray of beautifully crafted glasses.

"Champagne? I haven't had this since we left France." Isis sipped the bubbly beverage.

"Blakemore can get anything if you're willing to pay enough." Pierre puffed his chest. "But some treasures don't have as far to travel. You'll find his bar stocked with rum from my distillery as well."

They passed through the house and out into a courtyard lined with candles and trimmed in more flowers than Isis had ever seen in one place since the Garden of the Hesperides. Beside her, Circe bounced on her toes excitedly. "It's lovely."

"May I have this dance?" Rhys extended a hand to her. Circe set down her drink, and they joined the crowd of whirling dancers, her sister laughing as if she were filled with light.

"Only Circe can carry such joy in her heart. Look, she positively glows," Isis said through a smile. "No normal being can contain happiness like she can."

"Would you care to join them?" Pierre asked.

"Not yet. As you well know, unlike my sister, I'm

composed of more shadows than sunshine. I'm happy to observe from a dark corner of the room."

"I'm turning you into a scientist," Pierre said. "Observation is paramount."

He scanned the crowd. On the edge of the dance floor, Blakemore was speaking to a young blond woman Pierre didn't recognize, which was odd because he knew most residents of the parish. Or maybe he did know her and simply couldn't recognize her behind the red mask she wore. On the contrary, Pierre had no trouble recognizing the look of annoyance on Blakemore's features, despite his mask. Whoever the woman was, her enthusiasm for their conversation was not returned. Étienne was in attendance, dancing with his wife beside Viel, whose partner seemed bored to tears by his topic of conversation.

A hard nudge to his elbow brought his gaze around to Isis, who pointed with her chin to the left. He followed her line of sight. "Lucienne and Antoinette. They're here."

"Antoinette still looks human," Isis whispered. She turned her back on the two and moved in front of him, leaning forward to whisper in his ear, "But we best assume their hearing is anything but."

"Antoinette looks positively ill next to Lucienne. Strange, that was how I remember Lucienne looking the morning we found her husband."

Isis's large blue eyes widened. "It may be part of the process of transitioning from human to... whatever they are. Is Antoinette's husband here? The poor man is likely the next victim if history repeats itself."

He swallowed as Lucienne's eyes found him across the dance floor and focused on the side of his neck where her teeth had once sunk into his flesh. "Lucienne sees me," he said.

"Try not to make eye contact."

"Antoinette hasn't married," Pierre said. He'd overheard two of the nuns talking about it. "She's the youngest of the three, and due to her sisters' dual tragedies, the nuns haven't found a match for her. Publicly, they've claimed it is to allow her time to grieve, but it's common knowledge that no man will have her for fear the family is cursed. She still lives with the nuns, although she spends most of her time with her sisters."

Out of the corner of his eye, Pierre noticed Rhys coming their way. Immediately, his eyes sought out Circe, surprised to find her taking a turn around the floor with Gabriel Blakemore, and in lively conversation, no less. The man was actually smiling.

"Where's Circe?" Isis asked Rhys when he arrived by their side. Her position meant she hadn't seen what Pierre had.

"The dragon asked her for a dance. I didn't think it was a good idea to refuse, and you know Circe." Rhys cast a jealous stare in Blakemore's direction.

"Dragon?" Pierre asked incredulously, wondering if it was some new nickname for Blakemore.

Isis and Rhys exchanged looks. What was that about?

"I'll explain later, Pierre," Isis said to him, then turned a smile toward Rhys. "Have mercy on the man. She's coming home with you after all."

Rhys laughed. "Anyway, it was a good excuse to find and inform you that Lucienne and Antoinette Devereaux have been staring at you all evening."

"We're aware," Pierre chimed in, absently touching the cravat at his neck that covered his fading bite mark, until he realized what he was doing and lowered his hand again.

Rhys rubbed his mouth. "I have a bad feeling about this.

Why are the Devereaux sisters here, if not to cause trouble? Delphine is in prison. They're social pariahs. No one is speaking to them."

It was a good question. Pierre had considered that they were here to try to repair their reputation following Delphine's arrest, but they weren't trying very hard to mingle with the other guests. He looked again in their direction. "They're gone."

Isis and Rhys whirled, their eyes roving over the dance floor. "Do you see them?" Isis asked frantically.

"No," Rhys said.

Pierre turned a tight circle, his anxiety rising, even as the music played and guests continued to dance, unaware of the killers among them. "There they are."

He gestured to where Lucienne and Antoinette made small talk with the governor around the punch bowl.

Isis's eyes narrowed.

"Suspicious," Pierre said.

"Agreed," Isis and Rhys said in unison.

Their suspicions were confirmed when a scream sliced through the night.

CHAPTER
TWENTY

"Where's Circe?" Panic rose in Isis's throat as the crowd became agitated, everyone moving toward the scream. She searched the crowd. Gabriel was in a heated discussion with one of his servants, but Circe wasn't with him.

Rhys grabbed her arm and shook. "Something's wrong. We'll never get through this crowd. Use the shadows. We have to find her."

"Unhand her." Pierre glared at the place Rhys's fingers dug in. Isis nudged him gently, telling him with her eyes that she loved how protective he was of her, but she was all right.

"I'll find her," Isis promised Rhys, then backed behind the candelabra, out of the light. Dark tendrils raced along the walls at her command, searching the building for her sister. She closed her eyes, seeing what they saw. Circe came into view at the base of the stairs. She was huddled over a woman in servants' clothing. When Circe looked up as the crowd rushed in, the front of her dress was covered in blood.

"It's her! She's the witch!" Lucienne Devereaux cried to the governor, who looked on in horror. "My innocent sister sits in prison, and the true culprit is here, caught in the act!"

Isis gasped, opening her eyes. "Oh my goddess, Circe!" She started for the stairs, but the crowd was dense.

"What did you see?" Pierre asked.

"Isis?" Rhys was pale now, his hands in fists.

Pushing through the crowd, Isis took an elbow to the chest and heard a curt, "Excuse me" from a man on the right.

"I need to get to my sister," she said, but no one was paying any attention to her.

Suddenly, a hand landed on her waist, and she looked up into the face of the dragon. Gabriel motioned to Pierre and Rhys. "Follow me."

He guided them in the opposite direction as the crowd, through a narrow hallway at the back of the residence and out the front door.

"But my sister!" Isis protested.

"Your sister is being taken to prison," Gabriel said.

"What?" Rhys's expression turned positively violent. "Why?"

"She was found hovering over the body of my maid." Gabriel growled. "There was blood on your wife's dress, and as my maid had been drained of all her blood, assumptions were made."

"You were dancing with her! What happened?" Rhys asked.

"One of my staff approached her while we were dancing and said a message had arrived for her. He led her away. I assume that's when my maid was killed. He has no memory of the incident."

"Circe is not a vampire," Isis said incredulously.

"But she was framed by one," Gabriel said softly. "I must get back to my guests before my absence is noticed. Go. Be with your sister."

Pierre gathered her into his arms. "I'll talk to Étienne. He's a friend. Maybe..."

Rhys took Isis's arm. "Let's go."

IN THE MIDDLE OF THE NIGHT, ONCE THE GUARDS HAD FALLEN asleep, Isis transported herself to Circe, finding her sister huddled in the corner of a dank and filthy cell, her usual sunshine replaced by a flood of tears. As soon as Isis formed, Circe reached for her, mouth open in greeting, but Isis pressed a finger to her lips. "Shh." She pointed her chin in the direction of another prisoner asleep in his cell.

Taking Circe's hands in her own, she dematerialized, forming again in the salon at Tanglewood Plantation.

"Thank the goddess." Rhys pulled Circe into his arms.

Still clinging to her husband, Circe gestured to Medea to bring her Endora, who was fussing hungrily. She sank into a chair and started nursing the famished babe.

"You must be exhausted," Pierre said to Isis, his hands landing on her shoulders and guiding her to a nearby chair.

"It's been a long night, and I used so much magic," Isis admitted.

"Good work, sister," Medea said, handing her a glass of water. Turning back to Circe, she said, "Tell us how this happened."

Circe wiped under her eyes. "I made a terrible mistake," she said. "I'd been dancing with Gabriel. The dragon is an absolute delight and was so kind to me." Rhys grimaced like he had a stomachache.

"Dragon?" Pierre said. "I heard Rhys call Blakemore that before. Why?"

"Because he is one," Rhys said. "His kind can transform into dragons."

Isis heaved a sigh. "He doesn't know. Pierre, I was going to tell you. He's from the same realm as us."

Pierre gaped at her as if she'd just told him bees could do calculus. "Is there anyone left in this colony who *isn't* supernatural?"

"Plenty of people," Medea said with a shrug. "You for one."

When Pierre asked no further questions, Circe carried on with her story. "One of Gabriel's servants interrupted us and said there was a message from you, Medea, at the door. I thought maybe there was a problem with the baby. I followed the man into the hall near the stairs, and the maid stumbled through an open door and collapsed into my arms. She was covered in blood. I'd just lowered her to the floor when Lucienne and the governor, along with Antoinette—who'd gone from looking sickly to having the vim and vigor of youth—appeared in front of me, accusing me of murder."

Medea groaned. "Devious. They must have noticed I wasn't there and used it to their advantage."

"How did Delphine even know who Medea was? I never mentioned her name," Isis said.

Beside her, Pierre groaned. "Her name is on the land grant. I noticed it, along with Rhys's, when I...investigated the location of your plantation."

Medea leaned back in her chair, looking defeated.

"Well, that's it, then. We'll have to leave New Orleans tonight, before the guards notice Circe's gone."

Isis tensed, her eyes immediately darting to Pierre. He had a position here, a life. She couldn't ask him to leave it all behind for her.

"I'd follow you anywhere, *mon etoile*," he said, answering her unasked question.

But Circe shook her head. "Where will we go? Endora needs a home. We can't keep wandering from place to place like this. First we left France, then Haiti. If we leave here, what's to stop it from happening again?"

"We'll just have to be more careful," Medea insisted, but she looked as weary as Isis felt at the thought of moving again.

"What if there's another way?" Pierre asked.

They all turned to look at him.

"Governor Perier is a personal friend. I could talk to him —convey Circe's side of the story. I might be able to convince him he has the wrong woman."

"Do you think that could work?" Circe asked.

"He's a reasonable man. If we convinced Blakemore to have his servant back up the story, even if he doesn't remember—"

"I can make him remember," Isis said.

Pierre rubbed the back of his neck, no doubt trying to quiet the tingle of unease at the idea. He seemed to make his peace with it. "Étienne is a reasonable man. He might find a way to release her."

Isis exchanged looks with her sisters and Rhys. "If there's a chance, we have to take it. Why should we allow the Devereaux sisters to take what's ours? This is our home. I want to stay."

"Me too," Circe said.

Medea leaned back in her chair and released a heavy sigh. "There's only one problem with this plan. The governor cannot release Circe if she's not in that cell."

Rhys shook his head. "Medea's right. It's a terrible plan. You can't be away from Endora that long, Circe."

All of Isis's hopes and dreams for a better life went up in smoke as she realized they were right. Circe couldn't go back. She was breastfeeding, and Endora was so young. She needed her mother. Isis stared at the rug under her feet. They'd have to move on. It was their only option.

"I'll just have to go in your place," Medea said, folding her arms.

Everyone's eyes snapped to her sister, whose mouth had drawn into a severe line. There was a long moment of silence Isis could only ascribe to all of them trying to make sense of what she just said.

"Medea...*no*," Circe said softly.

"Why?" Medea stood and, circling her wand above her head, transformed into Circe's twin, complete with bloody red dress. "You may be the best at transformation, Circe, but you are not the only witch capable of it. I have no baby or husband. And if the worst happens—"

Isis popped out of her chair. "You can't go through with this, Medea. They could burn you at the stake!"

"They could tie me to a stake." Medea walked to one of the candelabras that lit the dim room and stuck her hand into a flame. "They cannot burn me."

Beside her, Pierre swallowed so hard Isis could hear it. "Why isn't she burning? Are you all impervious to fire as well?"

"No, just Medea," Isis explained. "She was once mated to a dragon, and when she carried his young, her blood was infused with dragon's blood. Dragons can't burn."

Medea waved her fingers inside the flame. "Completely invulnerable to it."

"Still... Medea..." A tear ran down Circe's cheek. "It's not fair to you."

Isis thought her heart might break, thinking about the sacrifice Medea was offering to make. It was too much. She searched for the right words to say, but her mind kept struggling with the inevitable lack of other options.

Removing her hand from the fire, Medea took a deep breath. "You all think this is a selfless act on my part, but you forget, one of you will birth the three sisters who will take my revenge on Eleanor." She pressed a hand into her chest. "The book and the key I hid in Ouros await the day that your progeny will end her reign. Your lives are more important to me than my own."

"We love you, Medea. Your life is just as important to us," Circe sobbed.

"Circe is right," Isis added. "You're wrong to think your life is less important."

Medea gave a shallow smile. "I don't fear death, sisters. Death is where my love and my son live, and I fully plan to go there one day. Now, this is my choice. Isis, you will have to return me to the prison. Are you strong enough?"

Tired, she may be, but if Medea could do this for Circe, Isis would find the strength to carry Medea. "Give me a moment, and I will be."

CHAPTER
TWENTY-ONE

"**Y**ou have the wrong person," Pierre insisted, beseeching Étienne. "Circe was with Isis and me most of the evening. She is most certainly not a witch."

"She had blood all over her, Pierre. She was caught in the act."

"Blakemore's servant can explain everything. The dying woman stumbled into her and died in her arms. She was trying to help her!"

"A likely story, but Delphine Devereaux claims Circe previously tried to poison her. She even provided me with the elixir. Delphine claims she suspected the witch, and so she never drank it." Étienne produced a basket from a cabinet behind him, and Pierre stiffened when he saw Isis's handwriting on a card hanging from the handle, signed from Tanglewood Plantation. Inside was a stale loaf of bread, some soaps, and a blue bottle of elixir. "We tested the elixir on a rat one of the soldiers caught. It died within the hour."

Pierre shook his head. "There must be some mistake."

Étienne frowned. "You're soon to be married, Pierre,

and anyone in your situation would defend his betrothed's family, but on this, take my advice. Distance yourself and your bride. Circe is to be tried today, and Louis Congo has been fetched to burn her at the stake tomorrow. The people are demanding it. The square is buzzing with talk of going out to that plantation of theirs to sanctify the grounds. They think it's the seat of her magic."

"Excuse me?" Pierre didn't understand. They had Circe. Why did anyone need to go to the plantation?

"The basket and the poison came from the plantation, not Circe herself. Some of the men claim that a witch can attach her soul to things she's touched. They've got a priest, and they plan to cleanse the plantation with fire and holy water. I tried to dissuade them, but you know how these things can get out of hand. Word is they're heading there today. My advice to you stands. Take your bride and distance yourselves."

Oh no! Isis was there, at the plantation. What if the mob took one look at Tanglewood and decided they were all witches? Pierre burst from his chair and strode toward the door. "*Mon Dieu*, we have to stop this."

"I'm sorry, Pierre. It's out of my hands," Étienne called toward his back, but Pierre was already out the door.

He ran for his horse, mounted, and raced for Tanglewood Plantation.

"How did they get through the wards?" Circe yelled to Rhys. They both watched in horror as the angry mob, wielding pitchforks and torches, walked straight toward the big house. Endora screamed from her place in Circe's arms, seeming to pick up on the tension in the air. Circe tried in vain to settle her, bouncing and patting her back, but she was inconsolable.

"It has to be demon magic," Isis said. "The night I rescued Pierre, Delphine clawed through my protective ward. She must be leading them."

"They can't find me here," Circe said. "I'm supposed to be in prison."

"Fuck." Rhys drew his wand. "They're almost here. We need to fight."

"Without Medea?" Circe said. "We will never win against a mob of that size."

"I have to agree with Circe," Isis said. "The three of us aren't strong enough, and there's Endora to consider."

"What do we do?" Rhys asked, peeking through the shutters barricading the windows. "They have us surrounded."

Isis smelled smoke. The porch was on fire. They were burning the house! "Pack nothing but the essentials. Meet me in my room. I'll take us somewhere safe."

Minutes later, Isis stood in front of her mirror, wand raised as smoke billowed around them.

"Why is the mirror showing us Pierre?" Circe asked.

Isis concentrated on her fiancé, who was riding hard and fast along the river. Pierre would know what to do. He'd keep them safe.

"Don't ask silly questions." With a flick of her wrist, Isis called the shadows to carry them away.

"WHOA!" PIERRE DREW BACK ON THE REINS AS ISIS, CIRCE, Endora, and Rhys popped into existence on the trail in front of him. He barely succeeded in turning the mount in time to keep him from running right over them. The horse stomped in irritation as Pierre dismounted and ran to Isis, pulling her into his arms.

"Oh goddess, Pierre! We were attacked."

His gaze flicked to Rhys and then Circe, little Endora in her arms. "Étienne told me. Delphine and her sisters are behind this."

"They're burning down Tanglewood," Rhys said.

Pierre cursed. He took Isis by the shoulders. "Are you strong enough to get us all back to my place?"

"I think so. It's not far from here." Shadows gathered, and in the next blink, he stood inside his courtyard. But the effort proved too much for his beloved. Isis collapsed in his arms.

"Allyette, bring water!" he yelled, lifting her. Thank God Circe, Rhys, and Endora had arrived in one piece. They rushed inside, and he gently rested her on the sofa.

Allyette came with a tray and almost dropped it when she saw Circe. "*Mon Dieu!* The witch is here!"

Pierre shook his head. "*Non*, this is her sister Medea. They're twins. *Les jumeaux!*"

Although she seemed to understand, she abandoned the room as if the devil was nipping at her heels.

"Will she be a problem?" Rhys asked sternly.

"No. I'll make sure of it." Pierre raised a glass of water to Isis's lips. "How do we stop the Devereaux sisters? Isis mentioned before that there might be a way to contain them on hallowed ground."

Circe patted Endora's back gently as the babe rested on her shoulder. "In theory. If their power comes from demon magic, they have a few weaknesses. Holy water can temporarily contain them. If the grounds around them were sanctified, we could do a spell to hold them there permanently. We thought about the cemetery, but we'd need to build a tomb big enough to hold the three of them. The spell requires a triangulation of symbols on the inside of the room."

"Why inside?" Pierre asked.

"On the outside, the symbols would eventually wear away from the elements," Rhys said. "Also, the spell requires their blood, and if it rained before we could activate it, we might fail at containing them at all."

"Blood?" Pierre raised an eyebrow.

Circe and Rhys exchanged looks, and then Circe started speaking like he was a small child. "In order to make a spell to hold an entity with unknown powers, you must fuel the containment spell with their powers. Delphine's demon magic obliterated our wards, so we know our power alone won't be enough to contain them. But if we leverage the power in their blood, we can use it as a catalyst for a new spell that turns their own demon magic against them."

He looked between them. "But you're confident that if given the right conditions, the three of you can do the spell?"

"In theory," Rhys said. "But there are a lot of variables."

Pierre heaved a sigh. Isis was more coherent now, and he urged her to drink more. "I know a place with a room large enough to contain them. A room surrounded by sacred ground."

Rhys poured some tea and brought it to Circe, then prepared his own cup. "Somewhere other than the cemetery?"

"The Ursuline convent. Specifically, the new building in progress, which yours truly is currently overseeing." He pressed a hand into his chest.

Rhys leaned forward in his chair. "It's on hallowed ground?"

He nodded. "The sisters had it blessed before my predecessor broke ground. But I'm the architect on the project now. If you contain them, I can build the rest of the convent around them."

Pushing herself up beside him, Isis came more fully into the moment. "This is exactly the break we needed. If we can lure them to the convent, we can contain them."

"Can you take us there to make preparations?" Rhys asked.

"I'll take you today." Pierre poured himself a cup of tea and took a fortifying sip.

Silence spread across the room. Pierre wondered if they were also thinking about what would be left of Tanglewood Plantation. He didn't bring it up, though. It was too sad, and the last thing they needed at the moment was to wallow in more grief. He simply said in his most cheerful tone, "Until this situation is sorted, you'll all stay here, with me."

They each muttered their thanks.

Circe raised her cup, her expression turning stormy. "Now, we just have to find a way to lure the Devereaux sisters into our trap, all while enduring our beloved sister burning at the stake."

TWENTY-TWO

I sis had to conserve her strength. What they hoped to accomplish today would take a staggering amount of magical reserves, and they'd be doing it without their sister Medea's help. The part that didn't sit right with her was Medea's choice to go through with the execution. They had a plan, but it was a tightrope she was walking. Isis could not resurrect her sister again if things went wrong. But Medea insisted it was the only way to appease the mob. As far as Orleans Parish was concerned, Circe would burn at the stake today, while her twin and her sister watched.

Bile rose in Isis's throat, and she pulled the brim of her bonnet down lower against the sun as she waited near the front of the crowd beside Circe. Near the crowd, but not in it. The other observers were giving them plenty of room.

Rhys and Pierre were together, preparing for phase two of their plan. They'd left Endora with Allyette, a risk they had no choice but to take. It was a hot, muggy day, and the crowds lining both sides of the street only served to further stagnate the thick air. Sweat soaked through the scarf around Isis's neck, but she dared not use magic to cool

173

herself. Not here. Not now. Not when she would need every bit of it for what they had planned.

"The fish has taken the bait," Circe whispered, her eyes darting toward her shoulder under the brim of her bonnet.

Furtively, Isis glanced behind her, barely moving her head. Delphine was there. She sensed the woman at her back like a wolf stalking its prey.

"I warned you, Isis," Delphine said under her breath. "I told you this town was ours. I gave you a chance to leave. Now, you'll watch your sister die."

"Asmodeus will tire of you," Isis said in just as quiet a voice. The humans around them were deep in their own conversations, but she made sure her voice could only be heard by supernatural ears. She stared straight ahead as she spoke, a whiff of sulfur telling her Lucienne and Antoinette had arrived. "He is the demon of lust. He never bothers with one woman for long."

"He's never bothered with you at all." Delphine scoffed.

"That's where you're wrong. Ask him. For years, he pursued me. I know him well, his dreams, his desires. Even demons have dreams. And I promise you, I am featured in his." She instructed the shadows to twist and tangle around the women and knew precisely when they noticed because Delphine hissed like a snake backed into a corner.

"Keep your magic to yourself, witch," Delphine said, loud enough that a few heads turned.

Isis called the shadows back to herself. "You must see how similar my magic is to his. We were once as thick as thieves."

"Once. Not now."

"True. But I know him, and I have something I know he wants, something he's searched a thousand years for." Now Isis turned to meet Delphine's gaze. "If you agree to leave us alone and allow us to live our lives here, Pierre too, I'll give it to you."

"Why would I want this... thing? What is it?"

"Have you heard of Augustine's chalice?"

Delphine popped her hip out, looking bored. "No."

"St. Augustine dabbled in both Christianity and Paganism. He imbued the chalice with the magical properties meant to make him stronger and more resistant to curses. It worked. With it, Augustine became immune to demon magic. This frustrated Asmodeus, and he took an interest in the object. He wants it, not only because it would remove a weapon against him from this realm, but also because he believes he can use it, warp it, and make his own magic stronger with it. He's searched for it for centuries. If you had it, you could use it to buy his favor. Already, his attentions have turned from you to Antoinette. Don't deny it. I know the way he works. Soon, he will abandon all three of you, and your powers will fade."

The way Delphine's scowl deepened was encouraging. Her barb had hit home. To be sure, it was a guess on her part. She'd never been Asmodeus's lover, but her gut told her that the demon of lust would steer clear of monogamy and become easily bored.

Delphine's eyes narrowed, and her sisters whispered to each other and then into her ear. "You're lying. Even if you had this chalice, you'd never give it to me."

"That's where you're wrong. I love Pierre. The banns have been posted. I don't want to leave la Nouvelle-Orléans. But you've won. I can't stay without your permission, and Pierre will never be safe without your promise of protection. I will gladly trade the chalice for these things."

Expression turning icy, Delphine shook her head and jutted her chin toward the stake. Through a cruel smile, she said, "All this talk of chalices and demons, when all I want to do is watch your sister burn."

Isis turned her attention back to the stake and took Circe's hand.

That went well, her sister mused to her over their bond.

I have her exactly where I want her.

Military drums started at the end of the street, and Isis leaned forward to see Circe—or rather, Medea disguised as Circe—come into view, dressed in a plain white shift. Her hands were bound, and the executioner, former slave Louis Congo, prodded her forward. Isis swallowed down a lump in her throat and could not watch as he positioned her on the platform and tied her to the stake.

I don't think I can do this. I want to grab my wand and rage against every person standing in this street, Isis thought.

Try watching yourself be tied to a stake and know it's your sister taking the fall for you. This is the hardest thing I've ever done.

Tears welled in Isis's eyes as Louis lit the fire. *I should have used shadow to break her out of prison. We shouldn't have let it go this far.*

And leave the Devereaux sisters to ravage the parish? This is our home. We could settle somewhere else, but our problems would follow us wherever we went. Beside her, Circe shook her head.

Goddess, the flames are rising.

Trust the plan.

Isis looked up at Medea. Her sister's screams cut over the crowd that had fallen eerily silent in the street. The illusion that made her look like Circe started to char grotesquely. But Medea's gaze told a different story. As their eyes met, there was anger there but not pain, not fear. And then her sister's chin bobbed toward the wood beneath her.

"What's she doing?" Circe whispered, then caught herself and sent her thoughts through their connection again. *It's as if she wants us to look at the fire. You don't think she wants us to put it out, do you?*

Isis stared into the blaze consuming her sister. Symbols glowed in the burning branches. Not just symbols, *words*. Realization dawned, and she squeezed Circe's hand. *It's the Tanglewood tree!*

Isis lunged forward, but a soldier grabbed her around the waist and dragged her back. "It's not the end for you, mademoiselle."

A set of female hands pried her from the soldier's grip. "I have her," Circe said, then guided Isis toward the back of the crowd.

"Goddess, no," Isis whispered.

"There's nothing we can do. The tree is gone." Circe pulled her into a firm embrace.

Delphine chose that moment to appear beside them. "Have you just figured out my sweetest surprise? When I led the mob to burn your plantation, I managed to chop down a tree on your property, one of a variety I saw you carrying when we got off the ship. Oh, it was smaller then, but the similarities were remarkable. An unusual tree and unusual circumstances. Now, it's kindling."

If Circe hadn't been holding her so tightly, Isis would have lunged for Delphine's throat. But her anger at the vampire was soon drowned out by fear for Medea. She turned back toward the stake. The flames were above her sister's head, hiding her from view.

"Isis," Circe said, "you don't think..."

No, Isis thought to her sister. *Medea is fine. We'd feel it if she wasn't*. At least, Isis hoped they would. It was too late now. Medea looked dead, but that was always the plan. Isis wouldn't be able to recover her body until much, much later. Goddess, she prayed she was right and her sister would be okay.

She allowed the fear and grief for what Medea had gone through to color her expression as Isis turned weeping toward Delphine and her sisters. "The deal is off. I'll go to Asmodeus myself and trade the chalice he wants for his promise to destroy you. You'll regret this day, Delphine. Remember, Asmodeus visited me first."

She took Circe's hand, and together, they raced for the Ursuline convent.

CHAPTER
TWENTY-THREE

I sis strode toward the bricks and beams of the convent, knowing Delphine was on her heels. If she hadn't wanted to lure the Devereaux sisters, she'd simply travel by shadow. They were running out of time, though. The sun was low in the afternoon sky. Not only were Delphine and her sisters weaker in the daylight, but they also most likely feared drawing the notice of prying eyes. But as soon as the sun fell below the horizon, their strength and their hubris would multiply.

Before today, Isis had felt confident that she, Circe, and Rhys could overpower the three vampiric women, but with the Tanglewood tree burned, she wasn't sure. She still had her powers, but the tree had always been a grounding force for her and her sisters, an anchor from which they could draw on the literal root of their power. Now, that was gone. The truth was, Isis wasn't sure how it would affect what they planned to do.

Isis approached the border of the Ursuline's property and whirled to face Delphine. Circe ran ahead, into the partially constructed building. They were alone here. Not only was everyone currently distracted with watching her sister burn, but they were also on the edge of the square, and the Ursuline nuns were living in a temporary building near the governor's residence while the convent was being built. No one was coming this way.

"Don't think I'm going to give it to you now, Delphine. You had your chance. As soon as that sun sets, I'm taking it straight to Asmodeus." She walked backward toward the building, onto sacred ground.

"That just means I have until sunset to take it from you," Delphine purred.

"It's three against one," Lucienne added. "And your sister ran away to hide."

"Terrible odds for you on an already bad day." Antoinette stuck out her bottom lip.

Isis scoffed. "Just try it. This ground has been sanctified. Your demon powers are useless here."

"She's lying," Lucienne said. "They consecrate a convent after it's built, not before."

Delphine hesitated, but Antoinette stepped onto the property. "So what if it is? I think we've just established we outnumber you, three to one. Didn't you mention that your powers were just like Asmodeus's? If ours don't work, yours won't either."

"I feel no different," Lucienne said to Delphine. "It was a lie."

Tentatively, Delphine stepped forward and joined her sisters, casting an evil grin when she discovered what Lucienne said was true. Isis held up her hands between them. "No. Please. Let's talk about this!"

The Devereaux sisters rushed her, but Isis ran, entering the building and racing for the back room. Footsteps pounded after her, but she ducked into the dark corner of the inner chamber, the four brick walls broken only by the door and the light from the unfinished second floor. By the time she reached the chalice at the room's center, her breath was coming in pants. She snatched the jewel-encrusted cup from the stone floor just before Delphine reached her. Lucienne and Antoinette rushed in after their sister. They gripped Isis by the arms while Delphine wrenched the chalice from her hands.

"I feel sorry for you," Delphine said, cradling the artifact. "You might have been Asmodeus's once. I know he wanted you. Now, you'll be nobody's." She darted a glance between her two sisters.

"I lied to you," Isis blurted.

Delphine tapped her foot. "About what? This bloody chalice? I expected as much."

Isis stilled and called the shadows to her. "No, about my power being the same as Asmodeus's. Mine comes from the gods, his from the underworld, which means, on holy ground, mine still works."

"Oh, Lucienne," Pierre called from the doorway, pistol in hand. "Remember me?" She released a hiss before he pulled the trigger and sent a holy-water-soaked shot through her heart. She crumpled.

At the same time, Isis commanded the shadows to carry her away. She disintegrated from Antoinette's grip and re-formed on the second-floor scaffolding.

Delphine leaped for Pierre, teeth bared, but he slammed the door in her face, barricading her in. Antoinette's eyes snapped to Isis like a predator spotting her prey. She bent her knees and leaped. The sun had not yet set, or she might have been successful. She barely missed Isis's toes.

"That was too close," Circe said from the plank on the other side of the opening.

"Quickly!" Rhys cried from another board positioned to her left. Together, they formed a triangle above the opening to the chamber. "We're running out of time!"

"*Myiménos!*" Isis flicked her wand, and symbols Rhys had carved into the brick walls around the Devereaux sisters glowed to life.

"What is she doing?" Antoinette asked Delphine in a panic.

At first, Delphine didn't answer. She looked at the symbols, then at Lucienne, whose blood was seeping into the grooves in the floor, grooves that made up a symbol. Her lips peeled back from her teeth. "She's sealing us in with a spell fueled by our own blood!"

Antoinette started to scream and leaped again, her fingers grazing the board Isis was standing on.

Isis raised her wand and began to chant. "Delphine Devereaux, I bind thee, to this place and to your sisters for all time."

The tip of Circe's wand glowed to life. "Lucienne Devereaux, I bind thee, to this place and to your sisters for all time."

With a flick of his wrist, Rhys's wand ignited, creating a triangle of light above the open room. "Antoinette Devereaux, I bind thee, to this place and to your sisters for all time."

Together, their connection grew stronger, the power multiplying exponentially, as they recited in unison, "Devereaux sisters, we bind thee, to this place and to one another, for all time."

Delphine growled and leaped, just as the sun dipped behind the horizon. Her fingers wrapped around Isis's ankle and yanked. Isis slipped, almost dropping her wand as her hip slapped the wood beam she'd been standing on, and Delphine's weight threatened to pull her down into the chamber. She clawed frantically at the board, her nails failing to find purchase.

Suddenly, a hand was around her waist, keeping her from falling. *Pierre*. He was lying on the board, his gun in his opposite hand.

He leveled his pistol on Delphine, who was floating above the floor in an unnatural wind. Her claws dug into Isis's ankle, and she hissed at him through fanged teeth. Pierre fired, the shot slicing through Delphine's neck and landing in Antoinette's chest behind her. Delphine's claws slipped from Isis's flesh, and Pierre lifted her back onto the board.

Scrambling to her feet, Isis steadied her hand, the light from her wand connecting again in the triangle shape with Rhys and Circe.

Together, they repeated the incantation again and again, the triangle growing smaller and smaller until it became a point of light between them. Isis stared down at Delphine as the spell took hold. She was cradling Antoinette in her lap, her blood mingling with her sisters' and filling every corner of the symbol.

"You will pay for this, Isis Tanglewood," she said through her teeth.

Isis smiled as the spell completed with a flash of bright purple. "Maybe someday, but not in this life."

Taking Pierre's hand in hers, she nodded at Rhys and Circe, turned her wand on the boards and bricks beside the building, and began walling them in.

CHAPTER
TWENTY-FOUR

I t was the middle of the night by the time the bricks and beams were in place and the Devereaux sisters and their new prison were hidden from human view, sealed inside the architecture of the Ursuline convent forever. Pierre assured them that the rest of the convent would be built around the room at his direction. Once complete, the grounds would be blessed again, before the nuns moved in, adding an extra layer of protection.

Isis understood that the demon magic the sisters harbored was powerful. In time, they'd likely learn to summon things and even change the size and shape of their living environment, but they would never escape. They were tethered to one another and to that geographic location for good.

Thoroughly exhausted, Isis, Pierre, and Circe returned to the place where Medea had been executed, anxious to know for sure that she had survived the ordeal. Rhys had returned to care for Endora.

"Bloody Hades, she's still up there," Circe said softly, staring at the charred form of a woman tied to the stake.

The street was empty now, but faint wisps of smoke still rose from the cinders under her blackened skeleton.

"Circe, some privacy, please," Isis said. Her sister obliged, surrounding them with a spell to hide what they were about to do from prying eyes.

"Medea?" Circe said. "The concealment charm is in place."

The charred corpse opened its eyes and said through nonexistent lips, "It's about time!" Black chunks fell away as flesh ballooned around the bones, swelling grotesquely before reaching Medea's full size. She shook off the rest of the illusion like a dog, silky black hair growing from her head and falling down her bare back.

A high-pitched sound came from Pierre's throat, and he covered his eyes with his hand, much to Isis's amusement. Of course, Medea was completely naked. Her clothing had burned away in the fire. Isis held out her sister's wand, and Medea walked barefoot across the coals to retrieve it. A dip and flick and a dress wove itself around her.

Fitting her fist under her jaw, Medea tipped her head, and a loud crack came from the region of her neck. "That's better," she said. "You would not believe how uncomfortable it was to hold that position. Pierre, you can look now. I'm decent." She waved a hand dismissively between them. "You can parade naked in front of me at a later date, and we'll call it even."

Pierre's mouth gaped.

"She's kidding, Pierre," Isis said quickly, then pulled Medea into a hug before allowing Circe room to do the same.

"We were worried you might actually burn," Circe said. "They used the Tanglewood tree!"

"The bastards," Medea said. "It wasn't pleasant, but I'm

okay. I still have my powers, although I feel the tree's loss like a growing weariness. But that's a problem for another day." She turned back to the stake. "What do we do about the missing body?"

Pierre cleared his throat. "The families of those executed often bury their own dead. As far as anyone else is concerned, we can say we buried your body in the woods."

"Words every woman longs to hear."

"You'll be even more pleased to learn our plan worked. The Devereaux sisters will never bother us or anyone else in this town ever again," Isis said through a smile.

"Then I say we retire for the night and find something to eat. I'm positively starving."

PIERRE LED THE GROUP BACK TO HIS HOME AND SETTLED CIRCE, Rhys, and Endora in a spare bedroom and Medea in another. Isis, he kept by his side, not wanting to let her out of his sight after the potentially deadly events of the day. When he'd seen Delphine leap for her, teeth flashing in the moonlight and talons digging into her ankle, it had sparked protective instincts he'd never felt before. Isis was a powerful witch, but she needed him. He'd proven as much tonight.

And he needed her. He loved her. He'd always love her. No matter what it meant for his future, his position, or his soul. He was hers.

Sliding his hand into hers, he led her back to his room and to the bed. "How is your ankle? Do you need a salve or bandage?"

She shook her head and lifted her skirt. "Rhys treated it with an ointment earlier. It's almost healed."

He knelt in front of her, massaging her ankle and calf. The wounds were indeed almost healed, but he couldn't stop himself from inspecting them anyway. He needed to touch her. Needed to know she was all right. Her eyes settled on the pistol still hanging from his belt, and he removed it, returning it to its box in his wardrobe.

"You were incredibly brave tonight, Pierre. It couldn't have been easy for you," Isis said.

He loosened the collar of his shirt and leaned a shoulder against the bedpost. "I should say the same about you."

"It's different for me," she said. "I have magic. I'm harder to kill."

"But I have a pistol and a woman to love, and God help any man or woman who tries to keep me from her."

This earned him a look hot enough to singe. She rose to press her lips to his. "You love me?" she asked, as if she'd never considered the possibility, despite their engagement and all the other times he'd told her before.

He ran his hands along her shoulders and then went to work on the strings binding the front of her gown. "When I pursued astronomy, I thought there would never be anything I found as fascinating as the stars, but their light pales in comparison to what I see in your eyes. Botany and horticulture held endless interest, until I tasted the sweet nectar of your lips and experienced the natural beauty of your body." He finally got the damned garment open and freed her breasts, palming one and flicking his thumb over its tight peak. "And I thought the pleasures of rum a pleasant distraction, until I was intoxicated by the feel of your flesh against mine. You are my greatest discovery, Isis. An endless fascination. My sweet secret of the universe and the deepest respite of my soul. It wasn't brave what I did today. It was pure instinct to protect my most precious treasure."

A breathless gasp escaped her lips. "The things you say. I will never tire of the way you love, Pierre, as if your entire being is devoted to the task." Pulling back, she undressed the rest of the way on her own and tossed her dress aside, before returning to face him completely in the buff. Lightning coursed through him at the sight of her full breasts, narrow waist, and the dark thatch of hair at the juncture of her thighs. His cock threatened to tear through his breeches. He had to have her.

He reached for her, hooking a hand around her waist and pulling her against him. Without her dress, she seemed tiny in his arms, small and exceedingly soft. Her evening primrose scent met his nose and drew him in. He narrowed his eyes on her. "You've bewitched me," he said playfully.

Fisting his linen shirt, she lifted it over his head, then went to work on his breeches. "I assure you, I have not," she whispered in his ear. "But what is love but its own kind of magic."

She sank to her knees, removing his breeches and stockings as she went, until he was as naked as she was. His cock jutted toward her, already weeping for her. She tipped her chin up, and those deep blue eyes met his a second before she fisted his length, pumping toward the base, and licked him from base to tip.

"Mon etoile—"

"Where I come from, this is how we worship each other," she said. Rose-colored lips parted and wrapped around his cock, her tongue swirling around the head. A groan that sounded more animal than human left his throat, and he tangled his fingers in her hair, thrusting to the back of her throat. She didn't seem to mind the roughness. Humming her pleasure, she hollowed her cheeks and sucked him harder. As she bobbed her head, stroking and swirling her tongue, he thought he'd never known such pleasure. The view of his cock disappearing into her mouth again and again sent his blood pounding in his veins. A tingle started at the base of his spine.

She seemed to sense him getting close and wrapped her hands around his legs, clawing the backs of his thighs. The slight pain was his undoing. One hard suck and he came apart, moaning her name as he braced himself on her shoulders and spilled into her.

Once the room came back into view, he helped her off her knees, knowing the worship she'd shown him must be extended in her direction. She was his goddess after all. His Isis. He backed her knees against the bed and coaxed her to the center of the mattress. Kneeling between her legs, he turned breathless at the sight of her dark hair fanning across the pillows and her pink tongue lightly brushing her bottom lip.

He leaned over to capture that lip between his teeth, then stroked her tongue with his own, tasting himself on her mouth. *Mon Dieu*, he might combust from the erotic thrill of her. He already felt himself growing hard again. From her mouth, he trailed his kisses to her ear, teasing her earlobe with his teeth before feathering more along her neck and collarbone. She arched, tipping her head back and thrusting her pert breasts toward his face. He obliged her, drawing her nipple into his mouth, sucking hard until she cried out. He gave the other hard peak a nip, noticing the way the pain followed by a lick of pleasure flushed her skin.

He applied himself to learning her, seeking her pleasure like the conquistadors sought gold. He skimmed his knuckle from her navel lower, finding her wet and ready. A man on a mission, he moved down her body, gripped her inner thighs, and spread her wider, glorying in the sight of her. His mouth watered for a taste, and he did not deny himself. He licked up her center, noticing the way she bucked when his tongue reached her cleft. That. More of that. He circled the nub there, lapping and sucking, paying attention to what made her arch and moan. The feel of her against his mouth, her scent, the way she panted with pleasure and fisted the sheets.

She breathed his name, her thighs clenching around his head as she found her release. He didn't stop until she reached down and pulled his hair. Gripping her hips, he rose onto his knees and pulled her to him, entering her in one hard thrust. She arched again, her body clenching, milking him, her gasps and moans of pleasure driving him on.

Sitting up, she wrapped her arms around his neck and rode his lap, her beautiful breasts pressing into his chest, soft to his hard. So warm, so wet. He cradled her ass and watched the way their bodies connected, the sound of flesh slapping flesh filling the room. Before long, the familiar tingle had begun again, and when she pitched over the golden edge of ecstasy, she took him with her.

Only after every wave of pleasure was squeezed from both their bodies did they flop onto the mattress and crawl under the covers, exhausted. He curled around her and drifted to sleep to the sound of her contented breath.

CHAPTER
TWENTY-FIVE

With Pierre's arms wrapped around her, Isis drifted to sleep as happy as she'd ever been. When she'd arrived on the shores of la Nouvelle-Orléans, she'd wished to one day find the kind of love that her sisters had experienced. Now, she had, and he had helped her vanquish their rivals. They were safe now. They could rebuild here. Everything was falling into place.

In sleep, though, she was surprised to find things far less settled. Red eyes glowed in the darkness of her dreams, and Isis found herself lying on the stone crag in the underworld again, the ambient red light shining on the city beyond. Asmodeus stood over her, morphing into the form of the blond man in a pale gray suit. He shoved his hands into his pockets and frowned down at her.

Climbing to her feet, she brushed herself off. "What do you want, Asmodeus?"

"You didn't have to entomb them, Isis. You have no idea how much effort went into creating them. Working with humans is such a chore. It's like molding the Acropolis out of seaweed." His lip curled off his fangs contemptuously.

193

"If you didn't want me to neutralize them, you should have told them to leave me alone." She folded her arms, her shadows hugging her sides protectively.

"Believe it or not, my goal in creating them wasn't to hurt you."

"No?" She huffed incredulously.

"No." He narrowed his eyes. "I have a feeling about la Nouvelle-Orléans. I like it there. There's a certain energy that I think will make it a lovely place to visit on occasion. I was simply getting things started. Establishing myself, so to speak."

The dragon living there was probably the source of the energy Asmodeus was feeling, but Isis wouldn't mention him. Asmodeus didn't need any help with his evil schemes. "Well, you getting yourself started cost us our plantation and caused my sister to be burned at the stake."

Asmodeus rolled his eyes. "Don't be petty. It wasn't as if she *died*."

Just then, Isis noticed a boy squatting on a ridge along the dark horizon beyond Asmodeus. No, not a boy, an angel. His fluffy white wings blew in the hot breeze, and familiar deep blue eyes studied her with marked curiosity. Something about his face drew her in.

"Asmodeus, who is that?" Isis asked.

The demon of lust whirled, but the boy was gone. "Who?"

Isis swallowed. "Never mind. I thought I saw someone, but I was mistaken."

He turned back toward her, moving closer and hitting her with a dose of his power. She braced herself for the thigh-clenching need the demon of lust could dole out like no other, closing her eyes against the onslaught. Power passed through her body, but what was before an almost undeniable temptation caused barely a ripple in her inner pool. She opened one eye, then the other. His cheeks were red, and sweat had formed on his brow.

"Is that it? You are off your game, Asmodeus." She laughed at him, although it might have been the wrong thing to do.

Enraged, he blew into her like a dark wind, seizing her waist and taking on his natural form, all horns, fangs, and thrashing tail. "You will submit to me!"

She looked up at him and grinned, then turned into a column of shadows and carried herself to the open space behind him. "No, I won't. You can't force me, Asmodeus, and I don't want you."

"But you want the power," he seethed through his teeth. "Your tree has been destroyed. You're mortal now, vulnerable."

"We've always been mortal. Witches live abnormally long lives, but they do not live forever."

"Without your tree, you will live a normal human life. A mere hundred years at the most. I could change all that. I could make you immortal again." He held out a taloned hand to her.

She shook her head. "Human life, huh? That's interesting. We didn't know how the loss of the tree would affect us, but it makes sense. The tree was a tether to the garden where we were born. Without it, we are truly citizens of the earth realm. Hmmm. I guess if it's between eventual death or being with you, I choose death."

The roar that came from him blew back her hair, but he did not approach her again. Slashing a hand through the air, he growled, "So be it."

Isis was yanked backward, as if falling from a great height. She woke with a start in Pierre's bed, breath knocked from her lungs. Without waking, he pulled her against him. Her breath returned in tiny sips at first and then deep draws. A normal human life. She drew tighter to Pierre and kissed him gently on the jaw. If it was true, she was happy. She wouldn't want to live without him anyway.

EPILOGUE

The day Isis and Pierre were married, it rained hard enough for the priest to mutter that the devil himself must object to the marriage. The winds rattled the shutters, and the skies became as dark as night. Inside, the church was cool and comfortable. Candles burned beside flowers that her sisters had brought in to decorate the space. It was a welcome respite from a summer of extreme heat and humidity.

Isis chose a gown of peacock blue, knowing how much Pierre loved the way the color brought out her eyes. Her sisters attended in gowns of a deeper shade of navy that reminded her of the night sky. Friends filled the small church as they exchanged their vows in the human tradition, and the governor himself wished them well.

Following their victory over the Devereaux sisters, Medea, Circe, Rhys, and Isis had returned to their plantation, but without the Tanglewood tree, their crops had died. Their house had been burned to the ground. They chose not to rebuild and instead sold the land. Circe posed as her own twin sister and went by their mother's name of

Alena when in public. She was never questioned. People easily accepted that there had originally been four Tanglewood sisters. After all, no one but Pierre knew the Tanglewoods well and everyone had watched Circe burn, seen her charred body hanging from the stake.

Rumors began that the Devereaux sisters had returned to France. No one questioned this, but then, people moved on every day from the colony. The harsh environment wasn't conducive to permanence, not even for Isis.

In 1733, Étienne Perrier was recalled as governor, and his replacement, Bienville, chose to reinstate the previous architect, Broutin, to Pierre's position. Isis and Pierre returned to Europe, where they raised thirteen children, all of whom had an interest in the sciences. They were deliriously happy until his death at the age of eighty-nine from natural causes.

Circe and Rhys established a tavern and inn called the Three Sisters. Over the decades, they had four more children. All the girls grew to have magical powers. The boys did not. When their children had children and grandchildren, some had power, others did not, but the tavern and the name Tanglewood carried on. Rhys served as an apothecary to the parish until he passed away at the age of ninety-three.

As for Medea, after Isis told her about her dream and the angel whose face she sketched for her, the three sisters realized why he'd looked familiar. They were almost certain the angel was Phineas. Medea vowed to find her son and regularly traveled between realms searching for him.

Medea found him decades later and taught him everything she remembered about her past, Hera's golden grimoire, and the magic that made her a witch. But no amount of magic could keep her from aging, and one day when she visited, it was for the last time. She'd grown old, and it was time for her to be with her sisters.

Ninety-eight years after the Tanglewood tree burned, Medea, Isis, and Circe met at the Three Sisters on what would become Magazine Street. Circe's daughter, Endora Tanglewood, and her husband were running the place with their three children. It was there that Medea, Circe, and Isis bound their wands together, the last existing pieces of the Tanglewood tree, and gave them to Endora to safeguard, for if their vision was correct, a day would come when three descendants would need them.

That night, they spent the evening surrounded by children and grandchildren, celebrating their ninety-ninth birthday since the day they had started counting birthdays. After a celebratory meal and a toast of rum to Pierre, Rhys, and Tavyss, the three went to bed. Lying side by side on the mattress, their knobby fingers tangled together and their gray heads touching, they left their bodies behind and traveled on to their next great adventure.

Over two hundred years later, in the 1990s, three very special descendants of Circe and Rhys were born and returned to New Orleans, where a certain dragon remained.

And the three sisters' prophecy was fulfilled.

THANK YOU FOR READING TANGLEWOOD LEGACY. IF YOU enjoyed this novel, please leave a review wherever you buy books. The THREE SISTERS trilogy of books are prequels to the TREASURE OF PARAGON series. Start the series with THE DRAGON OF NEW ORLEANS.

MEET GENEVIEVE JACK

USA Today bestselling and multi-award winning author Genevieve Jack writes wild, witty, and wicked-hot para-normal romance and romantic fantasy. She believes there's magic in every breath we take and probably something supernatural living in most dark basements. You can summon her with coffee, wine, and books, but she sticks around for dogs and chocolate. Her novels feature badass heroines, fiercely loyal heroes, and fantasy elements that will fill you with wonder. Learn more at GenevieveJack.com.

Do you know Jack? Keep in touch to stay in the know about new releases, sales, and giveaways.

Join my VIP reader group

Sign up for my newsletter

- facebook.com/AuthorGenevieveJack
- twitter.com/genevieve_jack
- instagram.com/authorgenevievejack
- bookbub.com/authors/genevieve-jack

MORE FROM GENEVIEVE JACK!

The Three Sisters
(Prequel to the Treasure of Paragon)
The Tanglewood Witches

Tanglewood Magic

Tanglewood Legacy

The Treasure of Paragon

The Dragon of New Orleans, Book 1

Windy City Dragon, Book 2,

Manhattan Dragon, Book 3

The Dragon of Sedona, Book 4

The Dragon of Cecil Court, Book 5

Highland Dragon, Book 6

Hidden Dragon, Book 7

The Dragons of Paragon, Book 8

The Last Dragon, Book 9

His Dark Charms

Lucky Me

Lucky Break

Lucky Stars

Knight Games

The Ghost and The Graveyard, Book 1

Kick the Candle, Book 2

Queen of the Hill, Book 3

Mother May I, Book 4

Fireborn Wolves

(Knight World Novels)

Logan (Prequel)

Vice, Book 1

Virtue, Book 2

Vengeance, Book 3

Printed in the USA
CPSIA information can be obtained
at www.ICGtesting.com
CBHW011555181024
16050CB00027B/214